"Quiet down, it's time for *Night Whispers*."

Around the room, conversations quieted. Mitch had never heard of *Night Whispers* and he couldn't believe there was this much stir over some radio show.

"What's it all about?" he asked his friend Paul.

"It's a sex show," Paul said with a grin. "Well, not really sex, I guess. Women call it romance or passion, but let me tell you, I hear Lady Love's voice and I just ache."

Ache? Paul ached? Mitch nearly laughed out loud at his friend's exaggeration until he noticed the man was dead serious.

"Laugh if you want, but I'm telling you, this show is great. This woman, she just...I don't know how to describe it. She speaks, and it's not just how sexy her voice is...it's that you almost feel like she's speaking directly to you. Teasing you. Inviting you."

Mitch raised a skeptical eyebrow at Paul as he lifted his drink to his mouth. A few slow, mellow notes of a saxophone underscored the prerecorded introduction, setting a lazy, relaxed mood. Then a smooth voice spoke.

"Hello, Baltimore. This is Lady Love, and tonight I want to talk about sensual pleasures."

"Oh my God," Mitch sputtered as he nearly choked on his beer. *It was Kelsey.*

find I'm just a boring, conservative bookworm.

Dear Reader,

Imagine the freedom of talking openly about your innermost thoughts and desires. Though you're alone, in a studio, talking into a microphone, you know that out there, in the dark, thousands of people are listening to you. Fantasizing with you.

Writing the radio segments in *Night Whispers* was, for me, the most exciting part of this project. Like my heroine, Kelsey Logan, I really dug down deep and thought about seduction. Of course, I also considered how a man like Mitch Wymore would react, listening to Kelsey each night, knowing she lives right upstairs and is someone he's sworn not to touch.

How long can any red-blooded man hold out when an audacious sexy young woman decides she has to have him?

It's a real thrill to publish my first book with Temptation, the line I've always read and enjoyed. Innovative, fast paced, fun and sexy, Temptation represents everything I love in a romance. I hope you find *Night Whispers* a worthy addition to your romance library.

Sincerely,

Leslie Kelly

P.S. I'd love to hear from my readers. Write to me c/o Harlequin Books, 225 Duncan Mill Road, Don Mills, Ontario, Canada, M3B 3K9, or e-mail me at lkelly@lesliekelly.com.

NIGHT WHISPERS
Leslie Kelly

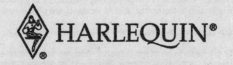
HARLEQUIN®

TORONTO • NEW YORK • LONDON
AMSTERDAM • PARIS • SYDNEY • HAMBURG
STOCKHOLM • ATHENS • TOKYO • MILAN • MADRID
PRAGUE • WARSAW • BUDAPEST • AUCKLAND

For the Tuesday night group,
I couldn't have done it without you.

And for Bruce.
Thanks for always being my pirate.

ISBN 0-373-25847-X

NIGHT WHISPERS

Copyright © 1999 by Leslie Kelly.

This edition published by arrangement with Harlequin Books S.A.

® and TM are trademarks of the publisher. Trademarks indicated with
® are registered in the United States Patent and Trademark Office, the
Canadian Trade Marks Office and in other countries.

Visit us at www.romance.net

Printed in U.S.A.

Prologue

"I WANT TO SEDUCE YOU."

The five words were spoken softly, nearly whispered, yet Baltimore heard. Throughout the bustling city, people paused, falling under the spell of the sultry declaration that seemed to echo in the hot September night. Patrons in a Harbor Place bar hushed one another. Riders aboard a city bus craned forward to hear from the driver's tinny speakers. Lights were flicked off in apartments around town as residents sat back in the candlelight to listen to her voice.

"Seduction. Even the word sounds erotic, doesn't it? It rolls off the tongue and instantly floods the brain with the images that most excite us. Gentlemen, what would it take to seduce you? Is it soft, white lingerie, so pure and innocent it's utterly sinful? Is it the flash of a woman's eyes that says yes, even before you've asked the question?"

It was ten o'clock and tonight, as it had been for the past two months, Baltimore was at the feet of a mystery woman calling herself "Lady Love." Near Charles Street a cabdriver flicked off his "available" light, slid his car behind a closed shopping center and settled in his seat to listen. A woman in a downtown row house lay in her bubble-filled tub, letting Lady Love take her away. Couples married twenty-five years turned off their televisions and looked at each other, feeling the spark her words always ignited.

"Maybe it's a touch. If she runs the tip of her finger across your bottom lip, will you be able to think of anything except how much you want to kiss her? If she feeds you succulent fruit, letting you lick its juice from her hand, will you want to taste more? When she so carefully allows her short skirt to ride dangerously high on her leg as she steps out of a car, will you want to push her back in and take her to a secret hide-away?"

Most of the men she was speaking to screamed a silent "yes" in their brains, picturing the infamous Lady Love doing all these things. They'd never seen her, yet each felt they knew exactly what she looked like...she was tall and short, a redhead and a blonde, slim and elegant and built with Mae West curves. They laughed and kidded one another, telling ribald jokes even as they fantasized about meeting her, wondering if she could possibly look as good as she sounded.

Women wanted to hate her for the effect she had on their men. But once they listened to her, they understood that she was talking to *them* even more than she was to their mates. In Lady Love's husky voice, they could hear their own fantasies and desires.

She had them and they adored her.

"And ladies, if he makes up his mind to make you desire him, can you possibly resist? If he stares deep into your eyes, and his breath comes faster across his lips, can you stop your body's response? If he kisses the palm of your hand and whispers 'I love the way you touch me,' can you stop yourself from touching?

"It's all about seduction. Making someone want you. Let's talk about it. I want to hear from you...tell me how to seduce you."

And, oh, how they wanted to tell her.

Baltimore settled back to spend four hours with their lady of the night, knowing now what she had in mind for them. They were never quite sure where she would take them when they turned her on. Some nights were light and playful, some heavy and erotic. She sometimes made them laugh, sometimes made them cry…but she *always* made them hot.

"This is Lady Love on WAJO…and you're listening to *Night Whispers*."

1

"WHAT HAS SHE DONE TO MY YARD?"

Mitch Wymore stared out his kitchen window and shook his head. Rubbing a weary hand against his unshaved jaw, he closed his eyes briefly. He'd just returned from a six-month research stint in China—his luggage still lay heaped on the floor in the foyer. He'd looked forward to returning to his brownstone, to his own huge bed, some real American junk food, and familiar surroundings. But this place didn't look familiar! From the moment the taxi dropped him off in his driveway and he saw the little red sports car parked in his spot, he'd wondered if he was at the wrong house.

It wasn't just the yard. The kitchen was changed. There were frilly yellow curtains at the window, and copper pots hung over the cooking island. The last time he'd seen them they'd been gathering dust in a box in the basement. A delicate-looking tea set perched on the sideboard. Pot holders and matching towels hung from a new towel rack. Fresh flowers burst out of a cut-crystal vase on the butcher-block table.

"Someone's also been messing with my kitchen."

Mitch didn't really expect Fred to respond. He'd been speaking more to himself than to his tenant.

"Yeah, looks nice, doesn't it?"

Mitch slowly turned on his heel and stared at him.

He didn't know Fred that well, despite the fact that the man had been renting the top-floor apartment in his home for the past year. Fred was a young grad student—serious, studious and quiet—the perfect tenant, and, frankly, that was just how Mitch liked it. They'd never socialized, and in the few encounters he'd had with Fred, he'd never seen him crack a real smile. Now a huge grin creased his face.

"Is there anything else I should know about?"

Fred's grin widened, and Mitch nearly groaned.

"Well, she painted the dining room, fixed the cracked chair rail in the living room, and repapered the foyer."

Mitch didn't have to ask who "she" was. Of course, it was Kelsey.

He glanced back out the window and rolled his eyes. The quiet little courtyard he'd left six months ago had been a nice blend of stone patio, a few rosebushes and a little grass. Two stately old maples provided shade in the back corner. Nice and easy. Low maintenance.

Now it looked like the pictures of those English gardens, a mass of trees, shrubs and flowers. A stone path meandered around clumps of evergreens and mums. Some green, palmy thing hung right over the gate and he dreaded having to circumnavigate it when taking out the trash. A huge mound of wildflowers surrounded most of the back patio. There was even a fountain splashing merrily near the fence.

He hated it.

"I'm gonna strangle that kid."

Tossing his keys onto the kitchen table, Mitch shrugged off his jacket and loosened his tie. All he wanted to do was strip away his stale clothes and take a forty-five-minute shower. Instead, he was going to leap into a confrontation with Kelsey Logan, the bane of his childhood!

"Kid?" Fred asked.

Mitch didn't pay him any attention. "I can't believe I was stupid enough to let her move in here. She's a menace, always has been, always will be. And she has liked nothing better than to irritate me since the day we met."

Fred seemed surprised. "I don't see her that way."

"Believe me, you don't know her."

Mitch wished he'd told her mother no when she'd called last spring to ask if Kelsey could rent one of the apartments in the Baltimore brownstone he'd just renovated. But of all the people in the world, Marge Logan was one he couldn't say no to. She'd done too much for him. He shuddered to think where he might be now if it hadn't been for Marge and her husband Ralph—in jail, dead…no telling. So he'd said yes, hoping the move would be temporary and Kelsey would be long gone by the time he got back from his trip.

"How long has it been since you've seen Kelsey?" Fred asked.

"Not long enough," he muttered. "Where is she?"

Fred pointed out the window toward the backyard. Mitch wasn't surprised.

"I'd better be on my guard. That monster dumped a bucket of fertilizer—*fresh fertilizer*—on my head once, just because her brother and I made the mistake of walking through her vegetable garden."

Fred laughed out loud until Mitch glared at him.

"I can't begin to tell you the number of acts of terror she's inflicted." Mitch mentally ticked off memories in his head of the times she'd run his underwear up a flagpole, hidden dirty diapers beneath his bed—and then there was the time she'd told half the neighborhood that Mitch slept with a stuffed bear and liked to dress her Barbie dolls up as Southern belles. Oh, the list went on and on. And those were only the harmless pranks. She'd gotten him into real trouble a couple of times.

Mitch had, of course, retaliated. He'd considered pounding her into the ground, and if she'd been a boy, and five years older, that's exactly what he would have done. Instead, he'd reacted by treating her exactly in the way he knew she'd hate most: he ignored her. It drove her nuts. He smiled at the memory.

"That was a long time ago, though," Fred said.

"Of course, fifteen years ago," Mitch conceded. "And I'm certainly not the type to hold a grudge. But I'm still going to strangle her."

Mitch burst through the French doors onto the back patio, wondering why he'd been surprised at what she'd done. He should have expected it. After all, her mother owned a plant nursery in western Virginia, and Kelsey had always spent more time digging in the dirt than playing with dolls.

Mitch stopped staring at the changes in his yard and took a brief moment to enjoy the slight breeze. It was an utterly gorgeous afternoon. Indian summer had stretched into the last week of September and everything was golden and glowing. The aroma of honeysuckle and apples floated on the wind. For a moment Mitch let go of his anger to enjoy breathing clean air.

The months he'd spent in China doing research for his newest book project had been difficult. Much tougher than he'd expected. The initial thrill he always felt when immersing himself in a culture he planned to study had faded quickly amid the crowds, congestion and rigid political policies of the country. In retrospect, the months spent researching his first book, a text on the ancient Mayan civilization, now seemed like a cakewalk, though he'd been living in a small jungle village that didn't even have a telephone.

Now that he was home, all Mitch wanted was quiet, solitude and privacy. He was ready to think, ready to absorb what he'd learned, and begin putting his thoughts on paper for the college textbook he was under contract to produce.

Fat chance, he thought. *Solitude* and *quiet* were two words he had never yet been able to associate with Kelsey Logan, the demon-child. He wondered how Baltimore had survived her presence.

Feeling a splash of water on his cheek, Mitch noticed he was standing directly in the path of a sprinkler. He grimaced, squared his shoulders and went to find Kelsey.

Mitch tiptoed along the stone walk and rounded a newly planted evergreen. Smothering a curse when he saw a little ceramic chipmunk, he restrained an impulse to kick it over the fence. Then he looked to the far corner of the yard and found her.

She obviously had been working. The pruning shears lay near some bushes, and a rake lay sprawled, spines up, across the lawn, just waiting for a Three Stooges-like accident to occur. Kelsey lay in a lounge chair with her back to him and he walked softly, being extremely careful to avoid potential mishaps with gardening tools. His shoes sank into the soft soil next to a leaking watering can. Glancing ruefully at the dirty Italian leather, he figured that was just one more thing to thank Kelsey for.

She didn't notice him. He was a step or two behind her, far enough that he cast no shadow over her face to warn her of his presence.

Then he stopped dead in his tracks. This curvaceous, voluptuous even, woman in the lounge chair could not be Kelsey! He'd made a mistake. Kelsey was the skinny, obnoxious, freckle-faced younger sister of his best friend. So he hadn't seen her in several years. She couldn't have changed this much, could she?

She wore a devil-red bikini, which was damp with the sweat of her exertions and clung to her skin. Her legs were slightly bent and raised, a golden honey color, slender and about a mile long. His gaze slid up, taking in the gently flared hips and small waist, then on to the trim midriff and the deep vee of cleavage revealed by the low-cut bathing suit, and up to the top of her sun-streaked hair.

He stared as she reached a slim arm over the side of the chair and felt around until her hand brushed against her cool water glass. She caressed the side of it, her fingers becoming damp and slick with the condensation, and she smoothed a little of the water over her fingertips. Then she reached into the glass to fish out a piece of ice, shook it gently and brought it toward her chest.

He swallowed hard. The woman—Kelsey?—moved the ice just above her flesh, and Mitch watched each drop of water as it fell in a trail along her collarbone. When she finally lowered the ice to the hollow of her throat, he released the breath he'd been holding. Then he slowly drew in another as she moved the cube down her skin, allowing it to melt on her chest. He heard her small moan of contentment at the cool relief and very nearly echoed it. The ice disappeared quickly until her fingers were moving over her neck and shoulders with nothing but the tiniest sliver, and then just a few drops of water. Her hand remained motionless for a few moments, lightly resting on her throat, and he thought she'd perhaps fallen asleep. He considered backing up and retreating into the house, but she shifted slightly, and he remained still.

No. No, this couldn't be Kelsey.

The last time he'd seen her had been at her high school graduation, seven years ago, back home in Virginia. She'd looked skinny and gawky and uncomfortable in the flowery dress her mother had made her wear under her graduation gown. They hadn't exchanged more than a dozen words that day, as Mitch had spent most of the time catching up with his buddy Nathan. She'd just been…there…little Kelsey the pest. When had she become little Kelsey the temptress? And where the hell had *he* been during her amazing transformation?

When she reached toward the glass, ostensibly for another piece, Mitch cleared his throat. He was not about to watch a repeat performance of what had undoubtedly been the most unconsciously seductive moment he'd ever witnessed.

"IT'S ABOUT TIME YOU SHOWED UP, Fred," Kelsey said, not turning around to greet her upstairs neighbor. She felt too warm and lethargic to even open her eyes. She'd been working all morning, wanting everything perfect before Mitch returned home the next day. She suspected he wouldn't be too happy about the work she'd done, but it was too late to worry about it now.

The warmth of the sun felt relaxing, not vicious as it could be in mid-July, but hazy and soothing, the way only an Indian summer sun in the mid-Atlantic states can feel. A light breeze blew across her body, and where the ice had touched her skin, it brought delicious coolness. She could lounge like this all day. But it appeared Fred had finally come to help out.

"I'd just about finished without you—you said you'd be down by ten. Are you still going to help me get this place cleaned up?"

Kelsey sat up and stretched a little. Arching her back, she moved her head from side to side to work the kinks out of her neck. If she didn't get back to work now she might never be able to. Her shoulders already felt achy.

"I'm going to pay for this tonight," she said, not even turning to face him. "My arms are killing me from lugging the wheelbarrow around."

Fred didn't say anything, which wasn't surprising. The man was incredibly shy. Until his girlfriend, Celia, had become friendly with Kelsey, he hadn't spoken much more than a half-dozen words to her. After that, he'd come out of his shell and the three of them had become the best of friends.

"Let me," he murmured very quietly. She didn't know what he meant until he moved behind her chair and put his hands on her shoulders. Kelsey scooted forward on the lounge chair, dropping her chin to her chest so he could rub the back of her neck. He worked expertly on her tight muscles, and she instantly felt better. Kelsey was a little surprised. His hands felt rougher and stronger than she'd expect from someone who spent ten hours a day in a lab. He also pressed and stroked with complete confidence, not typical for a guy who seemed so shy around women.

"Wow," she said with a lazy drawl, "I think you have a future as a masseur."

He still didn't say anything. She didn't mind. Fred was sturdy and dependable, a little too serious, but a great neighbor. He minded his own business and yet always let her know she could call on him if needed. She hoped Mitch's return tomorrow wouldn't upset the peaceful balance they'd created in the brownstone.

Mitch didn't know what crazy impulse made him reach out to massage Kelsey's shoulders. He'd been about to confront her when his hands had moved with a mind of their own. And once he'd started, he'd been no more able to stop than a flower could resist turning up to the sun. So he kept touching her, kneading her flesh, rubbing the golden skin, which felt smoother than the silks he'd touched in China. He had an overwhelming urge to kiss the base of her neck, and only her next question stopped him.

"So what time do you think Mitch will be home tomorrow?"

What was he doing? This was Kelsey! He'd known that, consciously, from the moment she started speaking. He recognized the slight Virginia drawl and the deep voice she'd inherited from her mother. When she was little, Kelsey used to get mad when her family teased her that she sounded like a boy. But she had most definitely grown into it. She sounded the way Mitch thought velvet soaked in whiskey would sound, if it could make noise.

"His high holiness isn't going to be pleased about the yard."

Kelsey had started calling him "his high holiness" the very first summer he'd come to stay with her family, since she'd had to share her room with the baby so

Mitch could bunk with Nathan. She'd put peanut butter between his toes the very first night! He shook off the seductive spell he'd been under. This was Kelsey. This was no temptress. He stood up and backed a step away from the chair.

"Do you think we should kowtow when he gets back? I bet he loved being in China where everyone bowed to him."

He didn't question the impulse. Grinning evilly, Mitch bent down, picked up the large watering can and dumped the contents all over her head.

When the dirty water hit her, Kelsey shrieked, then leaped up with laughter on her lips. "You rat," she said as she shook off the moisture, spraying him with several drops.

Mitch watched her glance over her shoulder and saw the smile fade from her face as she recognized him. When she turned around, he tried not to stare. He really tried. And failed miserably.

Kelsey, the ten-year-old monster, was long gone. Kelsey, the scrawny freckle-faced teenager, had disappeared, too. Here was Kelsey the beauty. The sharp angles of her face had softened with maturity and the freckles had faded into the creamy skin. Her sun-streaked honey-colored hair brushed the curves of her breasts, which were barely covered by the red bikini top. Her eyes were the same brilliant green as her father's, and her mouth, which he'd longed to slug at least two dozen times in his youth, was generous and eminently kissable.

Damn.

"Hello, Mitch," Kelsey finally managed to whisper.

What was he doing here? He was a day early, and Kelsey was not at all prepared to greet her new landlord in her bathing suit. Mitch had looked at her like a bratty little kid for so many years, she'd planned to be smartly dressed, cultured, urbane and adult when they finally met again. How typical of him to come back early and spoil everything.

"We weren't expecting you until tomorrow." Her voice cracked and she cursed herself for being a coward.

"I can see that," Mitch said. "Been doing a little gardening, hmm?"

He didn't sound pleased. Then again she hadn't really expected him to be. But Kelsey ignored the warning tone in his voice and gestured around the yard. "It just needed a little sprucing up. Isn't it beautiful? Think of the garden parties you could throw here now."

Mitch didn't say anything. He just stared at her, leaving her feeling terribly exposed. She grabbed her T-shirt and yanked it on over her head, plucking at the ends to try to cover her hips. He still stared, and she realized how foolish she must look trying to cover up what he'd obviously already seen.

"How was China?" she asked inanely.

"Crowded."

He didn't say another word, just continued to stare piercingly at her, as if he almost didn't recognize her. Well, two could play at that game, she figured. She lifted her chin and stared right back.

She wished she hadn't. Mitch had always been too good-looking for *her* own good. His thick dark hair, as brown as mahogany, hung a little long, nearly brushing his collar. The breeze blew a lock of it onto his forehead, and Kelsey had a moment's impulse to brush it off. His eyes, which probably should have been dark brown to match his hair, were instead a deep midnight blue. The contrast was incredibly dramatic. His face was lean, with a slight five-o'clock shadow highlighting the sculpted jaw. She wondered how rough it would feel on her skin, then shook off the thought and glanced over the rest of him.

Mitch's six-foot form was lean and solid as ever and, even clad in a white dress shirt and tailored slacks, he looked athletic and muscular. Not bulky, she noted, but toned, with a runner's legs and strong rower's arms. He had played a lot of sports as a teen, she remembered, and he and her older brother Nathan had been the two best athletes in their high school. She recalled being in sixth grade, watching their basketball games, proud when her friends would giggle and whisper about Nate, but somehow annoyed when they did the same thing about Mitch. If Emmy Frasier could see Mitch now, she'd positively faint at his feet. He was one fine male specimen.

"Finished?" He gave her a slight, knowing smile.

"Are you?" she asked, knowing he'd done his fair share of staring. He narrowed his eyes. Kelsey decided to call round one even. But she knew from experience the war was a long way from over. After all, they'd been battling since they were kids.

Years before, Kelsey's mother had offered to take Mitch in while his archaeologist parents traveled. Mitch got in so much trouble the first summer for smoking, drinking and sneaking out, that Kelsey thought he'd be shipped off to military school, something his own parents had threatened. The residents in the sleepy little town of Billings, Virginia, just hadn't known what to make of a rich, big-city kid with a huge chip on his shoulder. But Marge Logan had a soft heart, and Mitch kept coming back. His visits eventually grew longer until he was spending most of the year with them.

Little Kelsey, who thought all boys were totally gross, already had her hands full with her two brothers. So she did everything she could to get rid of Mitch. Her pranks had been relentless, but for the most part he'd ignored them. The angriest he ever got was when she purposely changed the time on his watch and car clock one night before he went out. His date's father had been livid when his sixteen-year-old got in at two in the morning instead of midnight. It didn't hurt that the girl was the daughter of the mayor. That had been the end of that budding romance.

Kelsey's campaign of terror came to a screeching halt when she was twelve and realized just how handsome Mitch was. Suddenly it didn't seem so bad to have him around. She tried everything to make him notice her. But he'd never seen her as anything but a pesky kid.

Kelsey smiled slowly. He saw her as an adult now, though. She had seen the expression on his face in that first unguarded moment, and knew he would never see her as a child again. She raised her chin a notch and squared her shoulders. Oh, yes, he saw her as a woman. And he certainly was a man.

"Exactly what have you done to my home?" he asked.

Not "Thank you." Not "Hello, Kelsey, it's nice to see you after all these years, how are your folks." Mitch was spoiling for a fight. She couldn't really say she was surprised.

"I made some improvements." Trying to ignore the

tone in his voice, she bent to clean up some of the tools she'd left lying around. Her loose T-shirt slid up, baring her middle. "This house didn't even look lived in. How long have you had it, anyway?"

"Uh, I'm sorry, what?"

Kelsey glanced up to see Mitch staring in fascination at her bare midriff. He looked decidedly uncomfortable. She dropped her lashes and suppressed the grin threatening to spread across her face. Well, wasn't this interesting? God, how many years had she waited to see that look on his face?

"I said," she answered slowly, leaning even farther to retrieve the rake, "how long have you had this place?"

She watched his eyes shift again toward the thigh and hip she displayed. "Three years," he choked out.

"I was sure you wouldn't mind me sprucing up things a little," she replied sweetly. "I know how much you travel and assumed you didn't have time to make this house a real home."

Kelsey looked for something else to pick up, liking the purely dumbfounded expression he still wore. She started folding the lawn chair, taking her sweet time about it, and allowed it to brush against her legs. A spot of grease or dirt smudged her thigh. Rubbing at it with the palm of her hand, Kelsey slowly wiped away the stain, knowing he was watching her every move. His eyes were twin drills on her flesh. She savored it.

"Your letter did say that I could make myself at home, and should feel free to use the yard and kitchen, didn't it? I mean, the little efficiency in my apartment isn't good for much more than warming soup."

"Yes, yes, of course I said that," he replied absently.

"But I meant you could *use* the kitchen, not redecorate it. And what about this jungle?"

"Lovely, isn't it?" Kelsey pulled her T-shirt up to her waist and efficiently tied it in a knot. Mitch looked more and more uneasy, shifting back and forth on his feet and cracking his knuckles. She watched as he dropped his gaze to her bare middle and it was all Kelsey could do to remain nonchalant. She'd waited half her life for Mitch to stop treating her like a little sister. And now that he'd noticed she was a woman, she was not about to back down.

Mitch wanted to yank his shirt off and cover her from neck to knee. Obviously she wasn't conscious of her provocative appearance. No. Kelsey saw him as another older brother, or she wouldn't be so casual about her state of dress...or undress. Right now, though, distinctly unbrotherly thoughts buzzed around Mitch's mind like a swarm of bees.

He shook his head again. *Stop it*, he told himself, *this is just Kelsey, still Kelsey*. Closing his eyes, he began to work up the indignation that had somehow evaporated in the minute or two that he'd been mindlessly staring at her.

"No, it isn't lovely. It's a pain in the neck. I had the yard exactly the way it was because I travel so much and I'm not here to maintain it." He gestured with wide arms to the profusion of plants. "Who's going to take care of it? I'm already paying a fortune to the guy who mows while I'm away."

"I'll take care of it," Kelsey replied, tossing her hair over one shoulder.

"You? You're going to be gone soon, aren't you? Your mother said this move was temporary, and you'd be here only a few months. Just an internship to give you a little big-city broadcasting experience, right?"

Kelsey smiled a little. So he wanted her gone, did he?

"I've been offered a permanent job at the radio station here and I've accepted. I'm staying in Baltimore. Looks like we're going to be long-term neighbors, Mr. Landlord."

Oh, no. No, no, no. That wasn't part of the deal. Mitch had been able to handle Kelsey renting the middle-floor apartment when it was only for a few months and he would be away. But now…how was he supposed to stand having her right upstairs all the time…every day…every night? If seeing her T-shirt ride up over that smooth skin was enough to send heat rushing through his body, what would happen if he had to lie in bed night after night and imagine her slumbering, drowsy and sensual, just above him?

And, of course, there were the days to worry about. Kelsey was a whirling tornado, sweeping everything around her into her energetic world. Mitch had struggled long and hard to achieve some tranquility in his life, especially after his turbulent teenage years. His now quiet existence lent itself very well to his writing, which was technical, engrossing and required his full attention. He hated distractions. No way could they be roommates.

"Forget it."

"What do you mean, forget it?"

"I mean," he replied slowly, as if to a child, "forget it. Your mother said a few months and it's already been six."

Kelsey flinched, and Mitch saw a flash of hurt in her bright green eyes. She obviously hadn't expected him to react this way. Mitch mentally cursed his own lack of tact, wondering when Kelsey had gotten so thin-skinned.

"You're throwing me out? Why? I mean, I know we were never best friends or anything, but we certainly weren't enemies."

How could he make her understand without appearing to be a complete fool? He could not come right out and tell her he didn't want to live under the same roof with her because she looked as delicious as solid sin, and she was his best friend's baby sister and, therefore, off-limits. Nor could he tell her she was a major pain in the butt and he simply didn't want her causing trouble!

Then Mitch thought about her parents. If they'd tossed him out the way he was trying to do to their daughter, his life could have ended up very brief or very ugly.

At thirteen, when he'd first started spending a great deal of time with the Logan family, Mitch had been full of resentment and anger toward his parents for their neglect. Their need to constantly travel, to nurture their fascination for antiquities, had left him with a childhood full of nannies and paid caregivers. Mitch had convinced himself that no one would give a damn if he spent his teen years in self-destruct mode. If it hadn't been for Marge Logan, an old college friend of his mother's, Mitch would probably have continued right into juvenile hall, drug rehab or much worse. She and Ralph had given him what he really needed: a loving, stable home life. And their son, Kelsey's older brother Nathan, had become his lifelong best friend.

He owed them all. Big time.

Besides, he didn't want Kelsey living in some bad

part of town. She was almost like his own little sister, and he needed to look after her just as her family would expect. And that twinge of—what should he call it—desire? Hell, put the right name on it. It was pure lust. That had just been a fluke. He hadn't recognized her. He'd been out of the country for six long, celibate months, and she'd been the first attractive woman he'd seen when he got back. It didn't go any deeper than that.

"I'm sorry," he admitted. "I didn't mean that the way it sounded."

Mitch was trying to figure out how to put the situation right when Kelsey breathed a deep sigh, tossed her head and squared her back so straight that one thin strap of red slithered over her shoulder and disappeared down the front of her oversize T-shirt.

Desire coursed through him again. "Stay. Please stay."

Kelsey couldn't understand his quick changes in temper. His mood ran so hot and cold, it seemed she didn't know him at all, even though she'd known him most of her life. One moment he was staring at her as if she were the most beautiful woman he'd ever seen, and the next he told her to get out. A big part of her was tempted to tell him to go to the devil, that she'd be out tomorrow.

But Kelsey really didn't want to leave. She loved this stately old house, even if only one floor of it was actually hers. She'd made it her home. Mitch traveled a lot, they should not see each other too often. Still, she hesitated. What about that flare of attraction? There had been a definite spark, and even now, minutes later, Kelsey could still feel his intense gaze on her skin. But it hadn't meant anything to him, obviously.

He still saw her as a nuisance he didn't want under-foot. So what if he'd given her a second look? Since she'd bloomed into a woman, long after she had given up on such an occurrence, men had been giving her a lot of second looks...and third ones. It didn't mean anything!

As for her instant reaction to him, well, that wouldn't be a problem. She'd always thought Mitch was attractive, but had grown used to it over the years. His admiration gave her a little boost of plea-sure because she'd wanted it so much at age sixteen. It was a powerful moment, that was all. Not to be re-gretted, certainly, but also not to be repeated.

Besides, Mitch looked utterly exhausted. His move-ments were slow, and his eyelids drooped. She imag-ined his foul mood was caused by fatigue from a cou-ple of days of traveling across the world. That would explain his strange behavior since he'd gotten home.

He seemed to sense her hesitation. "You'll save me a lot of trouble. I mean, it felt weird having Fred move into my home, and I would hate to rent the apartment to a stranger."

Kelsey nodded, her decision made. "All right, I'll stay."

Mitch released the breath he had not even realized he'd been holding. "I'm glad."

"Me, too." Kelsey smiled brightly. "I promise, I'll keep out of your hair. And you will not regret this yard."

If the yard was the only thing he came to regret about Kelsey living in his house, Mitch figured he'd be getting off lightly.

2

"WHAT IS THE REAL DEFINITION of sexiness?"

Lady Love paused for a moment, letting listeners think about tonight's topic. She always opened her show with a hook, getting them interested enough to stay tuned even though it was ten o'clock on a work night. One of the greatest compliments she'd ever been paid was when a caller told her he always got in trouble for being late to work, because he just couldn't turn off her show until it ended every night.

"Sometimes people confuse good looks with sexiness. I'm sure all of us have seen photographs of the beautiful people of the world, or stopped on the street to watch some physically perfect person walk by. No question, physical beauty works to attract us. But be honest. Ladies, who makes your knees shake, your lips quiver and your heart beat like it's going to explode from your chest...a man so gorgeous he's prettier than you are? Or is it a man exuding confidence? The one who has that look in his eyes, that look that tells you he's undressed you mentally and already brought you to mind-blowing fulfillment?"

She took a deep breath, purposely exhaling across the microphone, knowing that, in apartments or cars around Baltimore, her audience was doing the same thing. She let the tension build, let them fantasize a little, then continued.

"Gentlemen, you know what I'm talking about. A perfect model type might catch your eye, but be truthful...she's easily forgotten. So what kind of woman gets under your skin, like an itch you can't quite reach? Is it the brunette sitting at a nearby table who eats a piece of fruit like she's making love to it? Is it the woman in the tailored suit, the one with the glasses and businesslike hairstyle, who's got a curve in her hips and a long, slow stride that makes your mouth water?

"Sexiness...not just good looks. Is it the walk, the sigh, the mouth, or the steady stare? It's all in the eye of the beholder. So, tell me what *you* see as sexy. Call me. This is Lady Love on WAJO and I want to hear from you."

Kelsey Logan leaned back in her seat and spun a George Michael CD that fit tonight's topic perfectly. Leaning back in her chair, she listened to the music and allowed the lyrics to enhance her mood. She studied the fluorescent tube light above her head and thought about her own definition of *sexy*. One male image came to mind—strong, confident, intelligent, with lips that made her weak just thinking about them. Lady Love's definition of *sexy* lived right downstairs from her. She smiled. By the time the song ended, Kelsey was well prepared for tonight's *Night Whispers*.

FOUR HOURS LATER, when the show was over, Kelsey wearily slipped out of the booth, nodding to the late-night deejay who would run the graveyard two-to-six shift. He barely looked at her. She sighed in resignation. The guy still hadn't gotten over the fact that the station manager, Jack McKenzie, had given her the ten-to-two slot for *Night Whispers*, even though she was a rookie intern with only small-town radio experience.

Kelsey still couldn't quite believe it herself. She'd figured, when she came to Baltimore, fresh off a two-year stint as the morning personality at a tiny little country-western station in Virginia, that she'd have to work hard to eventually achieve big-city success. She'd been as stunned as everyone else when she'd received instant rave reviews after filling in for a vacationing deejay a few months before.

And it had all started with Mick Jagger's lips.

She still laughed when she thought about it. She'd been trying so hard to be good—trying to stay within the boundaries the regular night guy had left in his notes. Just spin the CDs, he'd said, no cutesy stuff, no stupid voices, no jokes.

Why she suddenly had the urge to invite callers to vote on Mick Jagger's lips, she'd never know.

It had been just one remark, one question. She'd just air-guitared her way through "Satisfaction" and, when it was over, had leaned into her mike and said, "What is it with this guy's lips? I can't decide...are they sexy as sin or repulsive as hell?"

Dozens of callers had flooded the phone lines, debating her question. Inspired by their comments, Kelsey had gone on to propose other provocative topics. And *Night Whispers* had been born. The show had begun airing in its regular slot two weeks later and she'd never looked back, never even paused to take a deep breath.

Every night, listeners clogged the phone lines, anxious to get on the air to talk about the sexy subjects Lady Love introduced. Brian, her producer, said it was because the city was full of closet exhibitionists who liked the anonymity of the radio. Of course, Brian would know about those things. He freely admitted that once he'd firmly slipped out of his own closet, he'd met plenty of flamboyant people.

Leaning against the doorjamb, she watched as Brian tidied his workstation, then tugged an expensive khaki raincoat over his immaculate silk dress shirt. The man's taste in clothes was remarkable. She'd never seen anyone, male or female, with as keen a fashion sense or as true an eye for color. He could, and did, wear every shade imaginable. Except, of course, for pale pink. Because, he'd explained, for a gay man, it was so redundant.

"Great show, doll," he said as he joined her in the hall outside the studio.

"Thanks, Bri. As usual, I couldn't have done it without you. Have you got Jack's approval for the rest of this week's shows?"

"Done. He gave me some grief about the erotica bit. We have to be real careful with the callers that night."

Kelsey shrugged. "When don't we have to be careful?"

Brian cinched his belt tight around the waist of his raincoat. "You know how station managers are...covering their own butts while we take all the risks."

She paused, giving him a sultry grin. "Taking risks is such fun, though, isn't it?"

"Absolutely, Lady Love. Absolutely." He hooked his arm in hers as they left the building.

KELSEY HAD THE NEXT NIGHT off and took advantage of the extra time to get some chores done. She stood in the basement Saturday afternoon, finishing up laundry while mentally going over some show ideas. She was completely lost in thought.

"Is it really necessary for you to hang your panty hose on the doorknob?"

Kelsey screeched and dropped the bottle of liquid laundry detergent she'd been carefully pouring. It careened off the corner of the washing machine, tipped end over end and splashed to the floor. A bright blue sticky trail led to a plate-sized pool next to her foot.

"You scared me half to death!"

Ignoring Mitch, she grabbed a towel from a stack of clean clothes on top of the dryer and began mopping up the detergent from the basement floor. He had surprised her. Kelsey hadn't seen Mitch very much in the week since he'd been home. She'd tried to be quiet, knowing he was sleeping a lot the first few days. Then he'd pretty much locked himself in his apartment to work on his book.

"You're using one of Fred's towels."

She didn't look up from her task. "Your point being?"

"You might ruin it."

"Oh, no." She sighed dramatically. "Oh dear. How will it ever come clean? All this terrible mess staining his towel. What could possibly be harder to get out of terry cloth than…laundry detergent?"

Kelsey peeked through her lashes at Mitch and saw the corner of his mouth twitch. His shoulders shook, and the grin widened until she saw the dimple in his left cheek.

"You're such a brat."

"Nice to see you, too," she said as she dropped Fred's towel into the laundry sink.

"About the panty hose…"

Snagging the offending items out of his hand, Kelsey stuffed them into the laundry basket and gave him a saucy grin. "Good thing you didn't come in a couple of hours ago when I washed my…other unmentionables."

"Wouldn't be the first time I've seen ladies' underclothes, Kels." He narrowed his eyes. "Yours included."

"I don't wear little pink unicorns anymore."

No, he didn't imagine she did. Mitch tried very hard to dash the image of Kelsey wearing a black silk teddy from his mind. But he failed miserably. It didn't help that he had been thinking about her in that red bikini for the past week.

She certainly wasn't dressed enticingly now. She wore a pair of faded jeans, torn at the knees, which had obviously seen better days. A thick, shining ponytail bounced with her every move. A huge cartoon mouse covered the front of her T-shirt. But she still managed to look incredibly sexy.

Mitch had been avoiding her. He could admit that to himself, not that he'd ever let her know. For days, he'd locked himself in his study, ostensibly working, but often just listening for her footsteps above his head. She didn't make much noise, and sometimes Mitch didn't know if she was even home. Except at night. She kept late nights. Her bedroom was right above his and he heard her when she got into her creaky bed at around three in the morning. It was as he had feared. Sometimes he swore he could hear her breathing and the rustling of her bedcovers as she made herself comfortable.

Bath time was the worst. Kelsey seemed to scorn

showers, but nearly every evening, at around six, she'd run a bath. From the length of time the water ran, he'd say it was a very deep bath. Soft strains of music would sometimes drift down through the pipes, and often an hour would pass before he'd hear the tub drain. Sometimes he'd close his eyes and picture her, with her hair up on her head and a few loose tendrils hanging down, leaning back in the claw-foot tub wearing nothing but a thick coat of bubbles.

"Carry this for me, will you?"

Kelsey pressed one laundry basket into his arms, then walked up the basement stairs with the other one. In the kitchen, Mitch set the basket on the table, casually lifted her slacks and started folding. She did the same.

"How's the book coming?"

Kelsey knew Mitch was writing a textbook on the inherent changes in post-Tiananmen Square China. His first anthropology textbook, which had just been released a few months ago, was already in use at various colleges. That had surprised some folks back home to no end. Many people couldn't forget his teenage reputation as the resident hooligan.

He shrugged. "Just scratching the surface."

"You know, I still can't picture it. You, a college professor and now a textbook writer. When I first met you, I figured you would do something adventurous or daring with your life." She shook her head in wonder. "It's just that, I don't know, you seem so different. I guess I saw you being something like your parents, the big-shot archaeologists, but more along the lines of Indiana Jones, whip and all."

"And instead," Mitch said with a wry smile, "you find I'm just a boring, conservative bookworm."

Kelsey eyed him speculatively. He might be able to fool some people with that reclusive writer bit, but she knew him too well. She saw the dangerous gleam in his eyes and the sardonic smile on his lips. The way he held himself, all coiled and ready for action, and the way his voice dropped to a whisper when he was angry spoke volumes. He might have learned some self-restraint, but inside Mitch Wymore there still lurked a potential hell-raiser.

"Yeah, right. And I'm a debutante," she drawled.

She read the laughter in his dark blue eyes as he looked her over, head to toe, his gaze lingering on the haphazard ponytail and the wisps of hair dangling over her forehead.

"Come on. What's the story? How did Mitch the bad seed end up like this?"

"Why are you so surprised? I've always loved reading, writing and researching. Never had much problem in school...at least not academically. I've inherited that from my parents." He pulled a chair out and sat down at the table.

"Yeah, yeah, I know," she muttered, disgust lacing her voice, "I heard all about it. Doctorate by twenty-six. Gag me."

He grinned. "You did ask. Anyway, I taught for a while, found I didn't much like being restricted by class schedules and grading papers. Writing seemed a perfect alternative."

"Yeah, but why textbooks?"

"Well, I'd been writing articles for journals, magazines, *National Geographic* and the *Smithsonian*, that kind of thing."

If anyone else had said something like that, they would probably be accused of bragging. But Kelsey had known him long enough to know that Mitch wasn't touting his accomplishments. He merely stated fact.

"Anyway, I called a publishing company to complain that they kept updating texts and raising the prices so high my students couldn't afford to take my classes. I made some contacts at the company, found myself asking questions about how these texts were written. Sounded interesting. I liked the idea of travel and research and writing, and tying it all together with academia."

"Think you'll ever go back to teaching?"

"Probably. I did give some guest lectures at the university in Beijing, since I was working closely with one of their professors. I might teach a class here next semester, just to keep my foot in the door. But thanks to a nice little trust fund from my grandfather, I'm not tied down to a nine-to-five job. And that's the key, because maybe next time the company will need something on the tribes of the Amazon and I'll be off again."

It all made sense, in his annoyingly logical way. She *had* always pictured Mitch ending up a world explorer like his parents. But their careers had cost him a real family life during his childhood, and had instilled in him a need for security. It appeared he'd found a way to do his adventuring in spurts, allowing him to also be the academic, the writer...the loner.

That was the part that bothered her. Mitch seemed very much alone. "Do you see much of your parents?"

"Not really. They're wrapped up in their newest project outside Cairo. But they were here last Christmas. It was the first holiday we've spent together in about ten years. I have to admit, it was nice seeing them." He chuckled. "I think they've finally stopped worrying I'm going to end up in jail."

Kelsey didn't know the elder Wymores very well. They'd always seemed very exotic to her, and when Mitch first started coming around, she'd envied him his world-traveling parents. But once she realized just how unimportant he felt to them, she'd thanked her lucky stars for her own homebody family.

"I'm glad you've worked things out with them."

Though he shrugged and maintained a nonchalant expression, Kelsey suspected he, too, was glad to have some sort of relationship with his only living relatives.

"I imagine you're getting a lot done on your book," she said, trying to lighten the conversation, "the way you keep yourself locked in your study."

"Lonely, Kelsey?"

"No, of course not," she insisted. "Actually, it's nice having the house so quiet. Fred makes almost no noise, which has been great since I started working the night shift and sleeping late in the morning."

"Night shift? Since when?"

"Well," she said, wishing she'd not brought up the subject, "two months ago I filled in for Mafia Don when he was on vacation. And it went over pretty well. It was my first shot on the air alone here, and I guess I did a good job. "

"Mafia Don's the guy who handles the evening rush-hour show, right? The one who always argues with every caller? I didn't realize you were working with him."

"After my internship, they offered me a permanent job at the station. I was just supposed to work with Dr. Hal, the shrink. He went kind of nuts on the air one day," Kelsey said with a small grin. "He started yelling at people, comparing their problems with his own. He, uh...got a little personal...something about liking to wear high heels and fruit on his head. That was his last day. So they temporarily expanded Don's show and made me his on-air sidekick."

"Kelsey Logan, the 'pay attention to me' queen, somebody's sidekick? I have trouble picturing that."

"Ha, ha, very funny. Anyway, Don was away, I filled in, got a great response, and they gave me a shot at my own show."

"Do they have you doing the world issues in the evenings?"

"Not exactly," she said as she quickly grabbed a shirt.

"What then?"

Kelsey finished the last shirt and stacked everything back in the empty laundry basket. Stalling further, she got a glass and poured herself some ice water, hoping he'd move on to something else while she slowly drank it.

Mitch didn't budge. He cocked his head in that irritating way and raised an eyebrow, as he always had when waiting for her to take her turn in Monopoly when she'd just rounded the corner toward Boardwalk and he had all the hotels!

"It's a new show, okay?" she said, finally. "Right now I'm just winging it. The topic changes constantly."

Mitch knew she'd been itching for a break on a big-city station. Her mother had said Kelsey had been a big hit on the local station back home. With her talent for impersonations and her quick wit, Kelsey was a natural performer. She had always said she'd be on

stage, TV, film or on the radio. Most times he'd just
wished she'd be on another planet.

"What time are you on?"

"Late night. Ten to two."

Mitch frowned. "You mean you're working until
two in the morning in a nearly deserted building in a
not-so-great part of town?"

"It's perfectly safe. There are plenty of people
around at night, including a security guard. And I
park right by the door. Would you please stop treating
me like a little girl?" she snapped.

Mitch bit back a retort. He hadn't meant to patron-
ize her. But he'd promised her parents she'd be safe
living in Baltimore. He hadn't been around to keep an
eye on her for the first several months, but intended to
remedy that starting right now. He was going to look
after her whether she liked it or not.

Kelsey saw the caretaker look in his eye and was not
in the mood to deal with it. No way was she going to
start explaining to him about *Night Whispers* and hear
his lecture about why she shouldn't do it. That would
come soon enough.

"Thanks for your help. I'll see you later," Kelsey
said as she tried to stack the two laundry baskets together.

Mitch grabbed one away from her and said, "Let me
help."

Kelsey moved toward the heavy oak door that led
into the hallway. The hall extended along one side of
the house, from back to front. She always used it to ac-
cess the kitchen and, of course, the basement laundry
room. Mitch, however, walked toward the other door,
which led into his living room. She followed him.

There were two entrances to Mitch's apartment, one

from the main foyer of the house, and the other from the kitchen. Kelsey had felt free to enter his private rooms to clean and decorate while he was away, but had not set foot in this area since his return. The first thing she noticed was the clutter.

"Good grief, have you put anything away since you got home?"

Papers and pamphlets covered the coffee table, and six months' worth of junk mail erupted from the top of the trash can. She figured he was using the living room as a temporary office because the room he used as a study was already crammed with books, papers and files.

"You need a maid."

"Volunteering?"

"Not on your life," she retorted. "I remember how you nearly ripped my head off when I was twelve and I tried to clean off that desk you and Nathan used to share."

"Don't go there, Kelsey. You purposely threw out a lot of my mail. And you tossed one of Nathan's songs."

"Well," she admitted, "I was getting a little sick of you rereading those notes from Melanie Thompson. And the day Nathan actually learns to play the guitar and write music will be the day I sprout wings and fly home."

"Thank goodness he gave up on that," Mitch agreed with a grin.

Kelsey returned the bright smile, thinking how unfair it was for a man to have those gorgeous dimples and sensual lips. She walked past him as he held open the door to the foyer with his foot.

Mitch walked up the steep wooden stairs right behind Kelsey. Watching her walk in tight jeans was a joy any man would want to behold, and he enjoyed every moment of it. He found himself wondering once again when she had filled out so beautifully. Before he thought better of it, he asked her. "Kelsey, when exactly did you change?"

She laughed lightly. "I haven't changed, Mitch. I'm still the rotten little teaser I was all those years ago. I've just learned some self-control."

"I meant physically."

She raised an eyebrow. "You mean, when did I fill out?"

Mitch nodded. He really didn't know why he'd asked her—it seemed stupid to come right out and admit to her that he'd noticed her looks. The woman was already too confident. "You're...so different than you were."

"I'm a late bloomer, I guess. Mom said she was the same way and she kept promising me that one day I'd wake up and not look like a Popsicle stick with a head on it. She was right."

She most certainly was. Kelsey was curvy and feminine, soft and supple. He found himself thinking about how perfectly their bodies would fit together, but realized he could get totally lost if he let his mind travel down that road. And the fact that he was having these thoughts about little Kelsey Logan made them even worse!

"Anyway, I realized I had 'arrived' when I was a sophomore in college and was out running. The captain of the football team ran into a goalpost when I went by. I didn't know why until my friends told me it was because he was staring at me."

"What did you do?" he asked. "Reenact the whole humiliating event for your dorm that night?"

Kelsey frowned. "I wasn't a ten-year-old anymore, Mitch."

"I'm sorry," he admitted, knowing he'd offended her. "I'm sure you didn't laugh at him."

She shook her head. "I should say not. The poor guy ended up with a dislocated shoulder. I felt so bad I went out with him several times, and we had absolutely nothing in common."

"Poor thing," he murmured, "going from plain-Jane to queen of the prom overnight, and forced to go on several dates with the captain of the college football team."

"Well," she laughed, "I guess it wasn't so bad at that."

Mitch looked around her apartment as they entered. He hadn't seen it since she had moved in and had to admit it looked great. Kelsey's talent with plants was evidenced by the amount of greenery, and pictures of her family were everywhere. He paused to look at the latest photos of her parents, trying to remember how long it had been since he'd seen them.

A wicker patio set stood in a sunny corner by the rear bay window, and he walked around it to glance outside. "No wonder you work in the yard so much. You have the best view in the house."

Kelsey moved next to him. "You have to admit, I did a good job. Aren't you glad I took the initiative?"

"You always do. Jump first, look later," he said steadily.

"Like you used to." She dared him to deny it. He didn't try.

They fell silent and Kelsey suddenly realized just

how close together they'd been standing. She shivered a little as his arm brushed her shoulder. She could feel his breath on her hair, and she finally looked up into his sculpted face. He wasn't looking out the window anymore. Instead he stared at her intently.

A thick, dark lock of hair hung down on Mitch's forehead. Unable to resist, Kelsey reached up to brush it with the back of her hand. She couldn't seem to pull her fingers away. The moment stretched as Kelsey stared into his blue eyes. He had dark, sooty lashes that were too long for a man, and his lids lowered slightly as his gaze dropped to study her lips. She sensed he was thinking of kissing her. Kelsey wanted him to—at that moment, she was dying for him to— but he didn't.

Mitch drew in a ragged breath. Expectation filled the air, fueled by the unexpected touch of Kelsey's soft hand. A rush of excitement surged in his chest, until he remembered whose soft, feminine, sweet-smelling body he was reacting to. He stepped back and walked to the door.

"Mitch?"

He stopped with his hand on the knob but didn't turn around.

"Thank you for your help," she said softly.

"You're welcome, Kelsey."

3

A FEW HOURS LATER, Mitch still wondered how he could possibly even have contemplated kissing Kelsey. What if he had given in to his impulse and done it? Considering how much he'd been thinking about her, and how his body responded every time she was in the same room, he imagined they'd have spent the entire afternoon in bed.

Mitch indulged himself, imagining for a few seconds the intense pleasure they could give each other. Then he forced the mental pictures away. Because that was never going to happen.

It wasn't just that she was Nate's sister. And it wasn't just that she'd terrorized him for several years. Mitch had known since he was seventeen that Kelsey delighted in tormenting him because she had a crush on him. But he'd never let on that he knew. She'd basically been a cute kid, in spite of her brattiness, and he'd never have humiliated her or denigrated her feelings. Unfortunately, he wasn't the only one in the family who'd noticed how little Kelsey felt.

Mitch would never forget the conversation he overheard one evening many years before in the Logans' house. He'd come home early from basketball practice. Marge and Ralph had been sitting with Aunt Betsy, Marge's older sister, who was the nosiest, nastiest busybody he'd ever known. None of the adults in the kitchen had heard him come in the front door.

Mitch could still hear every word of that long-ago conversation.

"REALLY, MARGE," Betsy said, "I think it's shameful that you're putting your daughter at risk like this."

"For the last time, Mitch is not a threat to Kelsey."

Mitch froze on the stairs, shocked into silence at the mention of his own name. *Why would anyone think he was a threat to Kelsey?*

"That boy is a risk to any girl who comes in contact with him. I heard all about him getting caught in the Thompson girl's bedroom in the middle of the night."

"Oh, for heaven's sake, Betsy, it wasn't her bedroom, it was the family's pool house. The two of them went for a late-night swim. Weren't you ever young?" Ralph muttered.

"Bedroom, pool house, it doesn't matter where. The point is, that boy is trouble. Marge, I know you've got a good heart, and Mitch's mother was your best friend in college. But that doesn't mean you're responsible for him. Good gracious, he's practically lived in this house for the past few years! If his own parents can't handle him, why should they expect you to?"

Mitch held his breath while he waited for her answer. Even after spending months at a time with the Logans, he was still never sure if there would come a day when they'd decide he wasn't worth the trouble and ship him off to someone else—or to military school. After all, why should Ralph and Marge be any different from his own parents?

"Betsy, that's enough. Mitch is practically a part of

this family, and he's one of the most decent, honorable young men I've ever known," Marge retorted.

"Tell that to the Wilsons…you know, the ones whose car he 'borrowed' three summers ago?"

Mitch groaned, not surprised she'd brought up that old incident.

"He's different now," Marge said. "Mitch was very rebellious when he first started coming to us. As fond as I am of Carol, I have to say she hasn't been much of a mother to that boy. She and Richard are much too self-involved to have children. How could a child grow up in that atmosphere and not resent it?"

"That doesn't change the fact," Betsy said shrilly, "that your Kelsey is in danger. That boy is too handsome by half, and Kelsey is a pretty little thing. She wears her heart on her sleeve for him and one of these days…"

Mitch tightened his grip on the stair railing, astounded that even a spiteful, narrow-minded old biddy like Aunt Betsy would believe him capable of seducing a twelve-year-old kid.

"That boy would *never* repay our trust in him by abusing our daughter. If I am wrong about this, then I am absolutely no judge of character," Ralph retorted. "Any man, young or old, who would take advantage of a young girl who lives under the same roof, who's practically his sister, would deserve to be horsewhipped! And our Mitch is not like that."

He liked hearing himself referred to as "our Mitch."

"Now, this is Mitch's home," Ralph continued. "We trust him, and we love him. He is here not out of any friendship with his parents—he is here because he's part of our family. And unless you treat him with the respect he deserves, you can just stay away, Betsy."

Mitch was shocked at the fervent defense. Rushing upstairs to the room he shared with Nathan, he suddenly felt confident and secure that here, at least, were people who would always love him. People he would make proud. People he would never, *never* betray.

THRUSTING THE MEMORY of the incident out of his head with an angry shake, Mitch threw himself onto his living room sofa. Here it was, fourteen years later, and he was close to confirming Aunt Betsy's dire predictions.

Any man who took advantage of an innocent young woman living under his own roof was a scumbag. Kelsey's family would never forgive him for the utter breach of trust if he gave in to his attraction and got involved with his tenant. Hell, Mitch would never forgive himself!

So, it would not happen. Period.

"HE HAS A DATE."

Kelsey said the words out loud, talking to her own empty apartment. She shouldn't have been spying. If she'd been minding her own business she would never have had to see that gorgeous, perfect-looking blonde unfold herself out of her expensive car and mince her way to the front door of the brownstone. If Kelsey hadn't opened her apartment door and peeked around the corner and down the stairs, she wouldn't have had to watch Mitch greet the woman with a kiss and lead her into his apartment.

"Step into my parlor said the spider to the fly," Kelsey muttered as she sat on the wicker love seat and stared at the backyard in the fading light of early evening.

Kelsey had been trying all afternoon to forget about

those moments earlier in the day when she and Mitch had...connected. That was the only suitable word. There had been a connection, a spark. They had both felt it. And he had walked out.

She told herself she was glad. Being kissed by Mitch might be nice, a lovely moment, but nothing could come of it. They lived under the same roof, saw each other all the time. And it would be awkward to bump into each other in the kitchen pantry or anywhere else if they'd given in to an impetuous kiss. So it was just as well that kiss had occurred only in her heated imagination. It's not as though anything else would have happened anyway, she reasoned. She and Mitch were casual friends, almost like family, and a kiss was, after all, just a kiss.

Who was she kidding? Kissing Mitch would be divine.

Kelsey heard a high-pitched laugh from downstairs and punched her fist into the pillow she'd been holding. The woman sounded shrill, grating, and Kelsey could not imagine why Mitch would be interested in someone like her. Other than the legs, the hair, the body, the face, the obvious wealth and elegance, what did the woman have to offer?

"*Lead* me to your parlor, said the spider to the fly is more like it," she said sourly.

Mitch was, after all, ideal prey for that type. She really couldn't believe some long-legged, perfectly coifed female hadn't snared him in her web yet. He was talented, gifted really, friendly, personable, utterly drop-dead gorgeous, and single. And, oh yeah, wealthy. What self-respecting, husband-snaring spider could resist him?

Kelsey had no idea who the woman was, didn't even know her name. But she hated her.

"MITCH, YOU WERE GONE SO LONG, I missed you so," Amanda said as she draped herself upon the sofa.

Mitch watched her, not attracted by her languid grace, as he used to be, but instead somewhat amused. Amanda's every move seemed choreographed—she always managed to frame herself well. For a split second he compared her to the several other women he had dated since moving to Baltimore. He suddenly realized they were all just like her: lovely, elegant, confident and sophisticated. Why, then, was she suddenly so unappealing?

"I'm quite certain you didn't spend the past six months pining for me," he said with a dry chuckle as he poured her a drink.

"Of course not, you know me better than that. But the social whirl just palled without you."

He handed her the glass. "Did I miss anything interesting?"

"Billingsley's retirement dinner was diverting," Amanda explained after taking a sip of her gin and tonic. "And Fern Handley has been having a torrid affair with one of her English Lit students. It's all over campus."

Mitch shrugged. He could have been listening to a taped conversation from six months ago. Amanda sat on the board of trustees at Wilson College, where he used to teach. The college was a veritable hotbed of gossip and intrigue. Who was sleeping with whom, who would get tenure and whose research project would get funding were the only topics of conversation at the various dinners and parties. He'd tried hard to care about it all when he first started teaching, without success. He wasn't cut out for the petty intrigue of it all.

"When are you going to give your guest lecture at the college?" Amanda asked.

"I'm not sure yet," Mitch replied as he walked across the room. "I haven't even started thinking about that. I've got loads of documentation to sort through first. Right now I'm trying to finish up the articles I've been writing for the *Sun*."

"Yes, of course," she replied. "I've been following them while you were gone. You had the whole city in tears when you wrote about the orphan girls."

Mitch sensed the boredom in her tone. She wasn't the least bit interested in talking about his work. Amanda never much cared to stray off her favorite topic of conversation: herself.

He sat on a leather wing chair, swirled his drink and waited for her to get to the point of her visit. He was very patient, a trait he'd worked long and hard to achieve, and within a short time Amanda was tapping her nails on the edge of the sofa, betraying her irritation at his aloof greeting. Finally she walked over and perched on the arm of his chair, resting her fingers on his arm. He glanced down at the perfectly manicured hand, wondering if those long, bright red nails would last for five minutes in Kelsey's garden. Probably not.

She offered him a coy smile. "I did hope you might be at least a little pleased to see me."

He should have been. After six months of intense research and practically no social life, he should have been enticed by the kind of distraction Amanda had always been willing to provide. But he just couldn't muster the interest.

"Refresh my memory," he said. "Don't I recall you flinging a very expensive Oriental vase at my head the last time we were together? That was right after we 'agreed' not to see each other anymore, right?"

He watched her bright red lips tighten and pull down at the corners. She was so spoiled. That was another thing Mitch hadn't been able to handle while they dated. Amanda had never been denied anything by her father, and she wanted a man who would provide the same mindless devotion. Mitch wasn't that kind of man. And he never would be.

"Really, darling, I would have thought you'd have forgotten all about my little bout of jealousy. I just couldn't stand it that you didn't want me to join you in China."

As if that was what had broken them apart. Amanda's overreaction to the trip was the excuse for the breakup, not the reason. They'd only dated a few months, and never exclusively, because of Mitch's realization that beneath the polish the woman was shallow as hell. The attraction had palled long before the trip to China came up.

"I think you and I both knew that was never an option."

She frowned. She hadn't taken their breakup very gracefully.

"Possibly," she conceded. "But there's no reason two old friends shouldn't spend time together, is there? After all, I've so much to tell you…did I mention who we've lined up as a visiting lecturer for next semester?"

Mitch watched Amanda as she spoke. He saw her lips moving and heard a vague humming sound, but he really didn't hear a thing she said. For some reason he suddenly found himself wondering what Kelsey was doing. Was she sitting right above their heads with the fading sunlight catching the golden highlights in her honey-colored hair? Was she upstairs lying in the tub? It was nearing six o'clock, and he half cocked an ear to listen for the sound of water running. But there was nothing.

Until the knock.

KELSEY NEARLY TURNED BACK and darted upstairs to her apartment. But she'd already knocked sharply on Mitch's door. This was crazy. Insane. He was here with a date, and she was about to barge in.

It was purely impulsive. She'd been about to run a bath when she again heard the shrill voice from downstairs. Before consciously deciding to do it, she marched to her closet, yanked out a satiny emerald green robe and pulled it on. Skipping downstairs, she banged on the door without even forming one cohesive thought about her plan.

Mitch opened the door and Kelsey smiled brightly. She pushed past him into his living room, pretending she didn't see the blonde in the corner, whose jaw had suddenly dropped, and said, "Mitch, baby, do you have some candles I could borrow? I'm afraid mine are burned down to nubs and I do love taking a long soak in the tub with candlelight flickering on the walls."

Narrowing his eyes as Kelsey cast him a sultry glance from beneath partly lowered lashes, Mitch dropped his gaze to appreciate her attire...or lack thereof. She wore a silky confection that clung to every curve. The top gaped open, revealing smooth cleavage, and the bottom of the robe just kissed the top of her thighs. Was she wearing anything underneath? He had no idea, but damned if he didn't want to find out.

"Oh, gosh, Mitch," stammered Kelsey. "You have company. Please excuse me...." Kelsey stared wide-eyed at the woman on Mitch's couch. "I can make do without the candles."

She looked too innocent. That sweet "who me?" gaze looked as familiar to Mitch as the back of his own hand. She'd had the same look on her face years ago when she'd sabotaged one of Mitch's teenage make-out sessions. The little brat had strolled out onto the darkened back porch and nonchalantly asked him, right in front of his girlfriend, if he was sure he should be kissing, considering the problems he'd had with "those little sores." The girl in question had found an excuse to break up with him a few days later.

Tonight's intrusion was completely intentional, just as that long-ago one had been. And Mitch knew exactly how to beat her at her own game. "No, Kelsey, don't rush off. Stay. Have a drink with us. I'll find you some candles, *honey*, I know how much you relish your bath rituals."

Kelsey was confused by his reaction. Mitch should have been squirming by now, attempting to push her out the door, to explain a half-clothed female to his girlfriend. Most men would be in the midst of a panic attack.

But he wasn't. He spoke in a low, sexy voice of his own, sending shivers down her spine. Staring with unabashed appreciation at her legs, he didn't look uncomfortable or embarrassed in the least. He actually moved closer to her until she had to tilt her head back to return his stare. The intensity she saw in those deep blue eyes shocked her. The heat was palpable.

"Mitch," an intrusive voice demanded, "I think an introduction would be appropriate."

Mitch didn't reply right away. Still gazing intently at Kelsey, he gave her a slow, seductive smile. Kelsey could barely draw breath as her eyes followed the movement of his sensuous mouth.

Finally he turned his attention to the other woman, who Kelsey had practically forgotten was even in the room. "Amanda, meet Kelsey. She lives upstairs. You could call her my semisibling. The sister I'll never have."

Amanda seemed a little relieved at the description, but Kelsey was not. Semisibling? Sister? She'd make him eat those words!

"Really, Mitch, you shouldn't encourage the girl to run around your home half-clothed," Amanda said with a forced smile.

Mitch laughed out loud. "That's true. Young ladies shouldn't run around in their nighties, Kelsey."

Kelsey glared at him. She could practically hear her mother's voice saying the same words to her when she was eight.

Mitch had obviously seen right through her ploy to destroy his evening. She was determined to wipe that grin off his face if it was the last thing she ever did. Thinking quickly, she forced a serene smile to her lips and moved a step closer to him. "I'm so sorry I burst in on you like this." Her every word dripped with sweetness. "The candles really aren't necessary."

She smoothed the palms of her hands over her satiny robe as if straightening it, drawing his stare down her body. When she knew she had his undivided attention, she said, "That window in my bathroom is right over the tub, and it should be a full moon tonight. The light shines in at the perfect angle and makes the bubbles absolutely iridescent."

Her voice dropped to a whisper, the sultry, sexy voice she used on her radio show, daring him to resist her. "Sometimes on moonlit nights I lie there in the dark, with my eyes closed, letting the water caress every inch of my body. I use a fragrant bath oil and it feels so silky and delicious."

She was getting to him. Mitch was clenching his fists, and his breath came a little faster. She could see the pulse at his temple beating and knew he was gritting his teeth. She had to bite her bottom lip for a moment to avoid displaying a smile of triumph.

Finally, when she was able to go on, she said, "Then I slowly pour cupfuls of water on my skin. It's so amazingly erotic when you can feel the warmth cascading over your flesh, nearly kissing you, yet you can't see it. You have to give in to the feeling."

Kelsey closed her eyes as she whispered to Mitch. She knew Amanda was straining to hear what was said, and dropped her voice even lower. "There are nights when I want to cry at the beauty of the sensation. It seems a shame to have such an erotic experience when I'm totally...alone."

Mitch had been leaning closer and closer as Kelsey spoke, wanting to catch every word. The images she evoked mesmerized him. He couldn't have moved if someone told him his pants were on fire. All he could do was stand, helpless, woven in the seductive spell of her whisper.

"Well, have a wonderful evening, you two," Kelsey said loudly. "It was lovely meeting you, Amanda."

Mitch watched the bounce of her shining hair, and the swish of her robe as Kelsey moved to the door for her grand exit. Suddenly he realized her every word had been calculated to drive him wild. *Little brat!*

Even as he tried to push the seductive images from his mind, Mitch acknowledged what a great performance she'd delivered. Kelsey Logan had always been a heck of a performer. Unable to resist, Mitch brought his hands up and slowly began to applaud.

Kelsey had her hand on the knob when she heard Mitch clap. Glancing over her shoulder uncertainly, she caught Amanda's gaze. The blonde laughed nervously. Kelsey wished the floor could open up and swallow her whole.

Rushing out the door, she hurried upstairs to her apartment, cursing Mitch and his *friend* every step of the way. They were laughing at her. Well, she figured, she probably deserved it. What a fool she'd been! Slamming her door behind her, she leaned against the wall and took a few deep breaths to calm herself down.

It had been all she could do to present a careless facade and walk away from Mitch, when what she'd really wanted to do was touch him with her hands the way she touched him with her words. Intimately. Seductively. Erotically.

"This is crazy," she said aloud.

And it *was* crazy. Her joke had backfired. Even if her seductive words had affected Mitch, it couldn't compare with what uttering them had cost her. All she could picture were Mitch's strong hands, his beautiful mouth and his firm, lean body. She felt achy and hot, and parts of her body tingled with anticipation she knew was not going to be fulfilled.

"Cool it, Kelsey," she muttered, shrugging off her robe as she started running her bath. She'd stopped

fantasizing about Mitch years ago. It had been bad
enough when she was fifteen and he was off at college
and she'd imagined him putting his arm around her,
or, heavens above, actually kissing her! Now that she
was an adult, she knew exactly why her body tingled
and ached and why she felt warm in her most feminine places. She couldn't allow herself to have those
types of dreams about Mitch. Because if she did, she
might never be able to stop.

As she lay in the huge bubble-filled tub, Kelsey tried
hard to shake off the erotic images dancing around her
brain. When she closed her eyes, she could practically
see Mitch's hands reaching to stroke her beneath the
silky water. She could nearly feel his lips trailing
kisses on her throat. She could imagine her fingers
dancing over his supple chest, curling in the dark crisp
hairs, teasing him and urging him on.

She tried naming the fifty states, tried reciting the
Gettysburg Address, but nothing would drive Mitch
out of her head.

Finally, she just stopped trying and gave in to an absolutely delicious fantasy. By the time she got out of
the tub it was very late, her body was all pruney and
the water was chilled. But when she caught a glimpse
of her face in the mirror, Kelsey wasn't a bit surprised
to see the smile lingering on her lips.

4

"To MITCH WYMORE, who's successfully escaped a nine-to-five job. It's good to have you back, buddy."

Mitch smiled at his old college friend, Paul, who'd just made the toast, and raised his own glass. "Thanks, man," he said, then sipped his beer.

They sat in a crowded, trendy little bar near the harbor. It was a yuppie place, with lots of ferns, round unscarred tables and varnished floors. Jazz from the radio provided a little background noise, but mostly he heard laughter, clinking glasses and buoyant conversation. Spending an evening shooting darts, ogling women, eating pretzels and drinking beer seemed just the cure for what ailed him...

Kelsey.

Mitch hadn't seen her since her grand entrance into his apartment over the weekend. He'd had a hard time kicking the image of those long legs and sultry comments.

"Have you seen Amanda since you got back?" Paul asked.

Mitch grabbed a handful of pretzels. "She came by the other night."

"And? Details, details...come on, buddy."

"And nothing. We talked. She left. Period."

"You're kidding," Paul said in disbelief. "I ran into her a few weeks ago, and she started pumping me for information about when you were getting back. I got the impression she was going to give you a tremendous welcome home."

She probably had been planning exactly that when she came by the other night. But since Mitch hadn't even been able to pretend interest, especially after Kelsey's visit, a highly offended Amanda had stormed out.

"It's not that I'd tell you anything, anyway," Mitch said, "but in this case, let me assure you, there's nothing to tell."

His friend didn't look as though he believed him, but Mitch didn't bother to elaborate.

"Quiet down," someone yelled. "It's time for *Night Whispers!*"

Mitch glanced around and saw the bartender reach up to the sound system to crank up the volume on the stereo.

"Oh, buddy, you've got to check this out," Paul said.

"What?"

"This new radio show. Everybody's talking about it."

Around the room, conversations quieted. Mitch saw people shushing others, demanding they listen. He'd never heard of *Night Whispers*, and couldn't believe there was this much of a stir over some radio show.

"What's it all about?" he asked Paul.

"It's a sex show," Paul said with a grin. "Well, not really sex, I guess women call it romance, or passion, but let me tell you, I hear Lady Love's voice and I just ache."

Ache? Paul ached? Mitch nearly laughed aloud at

his friend's exaggeration until he noticed the man was dead serious.

"Laugh if you want, but I'm telling you this show is great. A lot of people have *Night Whispers* parties. Everybody I know is into it. This woman, she just...I don't know how to describe it, she speaks, and it's not just how sexy her voice is, it's that you almost feel she's speaking from her soul."

Mitch raised a skeptical eyebrow at Paul's eloquent words as he lifted his drink to his mouth. A few slow, mellow notes of a saxophone underscored the prerecorded introduction, setting a lazy, relaxed mood. Then a smooth voice spoke.

"Hello, Baltimore. This is Lady Love and tonight I want to talk about sensuous pleasures."

"Oh, my God," Mitch sputtered as he nearly choked on his beer.

It was Kelsey.

"We all know about the five senses, learned of them in grade school. To taste, touch, hear, see and smell are all such gifts. Gifts that many of us take for granted and don't stop to consider."

Kelsey leaned closer to the microphone, closing her eyes as she spoke. The bright lights in the studio, and the equalizers, stereo and sound equipment, weren't exactly conducive to romance or, tonight, sensuality. She had worked herself into her mood, as usual, with her bath. That always helped. She hadn't been exaggerating to Mitch when she talked about the importance of a long, languorous bath, and found that her evening ritual helped prepare her to come in and talk frankly about the subjects she covered in her show.

"Tonight," she continued, "I want to consider them. Sensuous pleasures are derived from everything that surrounds us. The soft petals of a rose brushed against the cheek, then its scent deeply inhaled, gives such delight. The sweet, slightly bitter taste of dark chocolate lingers on the tongue long after it's gone. The calm solitude and silence of a beach under a night sky interrupted only by the sound of churning waves, washing forward then receding, brings peace and tranquillity. And who can look at a masterful piece of art and not be moved by its power and the skill of the artist?"

Kelsey bowed her head as she formed her thoughts. She always planned her topics in advance, but often her words were spontaneous.

"All are sensuous. Anything that invades our senses, anything we see or smell, touch, hear or taste, that brings us pleasure, that invigorates our soul, is sensuous."

Kelsey paused for a moment, a purposeful hesitation. Her audience was half-hooked already. She just had to bring them home.

"Now let's talk about sexuality," she continued. There, that was the rest of the lure. They were listening now. She could feel it. Brian gave her a thumbs-up from his side of the glass-enclosed booth, and she continued with a soft smile.

"Some people think they mean the same thing. But they don't. Tonight we're going to discuss how they differ."

Kelsey cued the music that led into a cluster of commercials.

"Stick with me. We'll be back in a few minutes. I'll start taking your calls later in the hour. Until then, please come back and spend some time alone with me, Lady Love, on WAJO. I'll be waiting for you," she said in a breathy voice.

Kelsey leaned back in her chair. Brian was mimicking applause, and she grinned back. It was going to be an interesting night.

MITCH COULDN'T SPEAK. He sat, in shock, knowing but not caring that he probably looked like an utter fool, with his mouth hanging open. Had that really been Kelsey? Of course it had. He'd recognize that voice anywhere. And she had come right out and told him she was working the ten-to-two shift. No wonder she hadn't wanted to talk more about her job.

"She got to you, didn't she?" Paul said with a knowing grin. "Did I tell you, or what?"

Mitch just nodded.

Around the bar, voices picked back up, and he caught snatches of conversation from other tables, most of it about Kelsey…Lady Love. There seemed to be universal approval and interest.

"Is she always like this?" Mitch finally asked.

"Uh-hmm, but it gets better. That was just her introduction."

Mitch frowned. Glancing around at the grins of most of the male patrons, he knew Kelsey had already all but seduced half the men in the place. Exactly how far would she go on this show?

"Is this X-rated, or what?" he asked, not really knowing if he wanted the answer.

"No, man, it's not like that. She never gets raunchy, and I guess she's got her callers on a time delay, because none of them do, either. Sometimes people try to steer the conversation, but she never goes for that. She's classy, but, oh, so sexy."

Mitch should have been relieved, but he wasn't. So what if she wasn't exactly pornographic? She was on the radio broadcasting to thousands, maybe hundreds of thousands, about intimacy and sex as if she were an expert on the subject. He hadn't figured she was a virgin, but he'd never considered her a sex expert, either. Hell, as far as he knew, Kelsey had never even had a serious relationship.

"I'd love to see what she looks like," Paul said, "but she could be a sixty-year-old grandmother."

A man staggering by must have heard Paul's comment, because he paused at their table, saying, "No, I heard she's a babe. A friend of mine parked outside the radio station one night and watched her come out. He says she's as hot as she sounds."

Oh, great. As Mitch had feared, Kelsey's show attracted psychos who were lying in wait for her outside the station in the middle of the night. What on earth was she thinking? Kelsey had always been free spirited, but she'd never been stupid.

The obviously drunk man leaned toward Paul and Mitch and leered. "I'm goin' down there myself one o' these nights. Gonna give Lady Love some real interestin' topics…give that lady lots to talk about."

Standing immediately, Mitch kicked his chair back and grabbed the drunk by the front of his shirt. He yanked the other man's face toward his, smelling the reek of too many beers. "You better watch your filthy mouth."

The man took a few steps back, nearly tripping over his own feet in his haste. "What is she, your sister or somethin'?"

Mitch shook his head, then looked around at the stares he was receiving. Paul gaped at him, as well, but Mitch couldn't begin to explain. How did he possibly explain about Kelsey? *Hey, folks, Lady Love's liv-*

ing in my house, sleeping right above my head, as a matter of fact, and you know the funny thing? She likes to eat peanut butter and marshmallow sandwiches with sliced bananas. And hey, get this, she once put my underwear in the freezer!

Mitch shook his head quickly, not quite believing he'd had the urge to punch out a loudmouthed drunk in a bar. He hadn't thrown a punch at anyone since he was in high school. When he thought about it, he remembered that Kelsey had been responsible for that fight, too! She'd told Mitch that she was secretly sneaking out to meet an eighteen-year-old, and Mitch had pounded the guy after gym class one day. The little brat had admitted she'd lied only after he'd been suspended from school for a week.

Shaking his head, Mitch grabbed a ten out of his pocket and tossed it onto the table. "I've gotta go. Beer's on me. Thanks for the invite. I'll see you soon."

Outside, Mitch hurried to his car and jumped in. He cursed as he slammed the steering wheel with his palm, then took a few deep breaths. Before starting the engine, he thought about how close he'd come to violence. Kelsey pushed all his buttons, even when she wasn't in the damned room! His hands were shaking, and since he hadn't finished half of his first drink, he knew it wasn't the beer. It was anger.

"HELLO AGAIN, BALTIMORE. Thanks for sticking with me. This is Lady Love on WAJO, and you're listening to *Night Whispers*. Tonight, we're talking about sensuality versus sexuality."

Kelsey paused, giving her listeners a chance to turn up the volume or curl up together on a sofa or pour a glass of wine. Or, perhaps, just roll up the car window to cut down on outside noise.

"Something can be amazingly sensuous, can give you immense pleasure, and have absolutely nothing to do with sex. And, unfortunately, many people go through their lifetimes having sex, feeling moments of physical pleasure, but never really experiencing the truly sensuous," she purred, drawing out each word to lend an intimate atmosphere.

Kelsey saw Brian waving and gesturing to the phone lines, and noticed that the switchboard was already lit up like Las Vegas. She wouldn't start airing calls for a while yet, but people were amazingly patient, sometimes waiting a half hour for a chance to get on the air. Brian busily screened them, getting names and a few words about what they'd like to say.

"The first step in understanding how sensuality can enhance sexuality," Kelsey continued, "is to understand and appreciate what is truly sensuous. To me, the most sensuous texture is human skin."

Brian gave her a quick grin.

"Rubbing lotion on my legs, letting it be absorbed, feeling my flesh grow more pliant, is incredibly sensuous. Not sexual. Now, let someone else rub lotion and knead and stroke my limbs...well, I'm getting a little ahead of myself," she said with a throaty chuckle.

Intentionally, of course. She tried all the time to jump ahead of the audience, get their minds working overtime wondering where she was going, then she'd go right back to where she'd been, teasing them, building up the momentum. It wasn't what she said that was so provocative, it was what she hinted at, and what the audience filled in with their own minds.

"Let's talk about scents. Smells are incredibly evocative. A certain perfume can take you back to another
time, and another place, and bring memories flooding
into your mind. For me, the smell of lavender always
brings with it sweet, warm memories of my grandmother. Closing my eyes and deeply inhaling the
scent of gardenias makes me think of lying in a garden, with the sun beating down on me. It gives me a
great deal of pleasure."

Kelsey smiled, remembering for a moment the afternoon when Mitch had found her lying in the backyard. She'd been feeling just such pleasures at that
point, enjoying the warmth, and the sounds of the
birds, and the smell of the earth she'd been digging.

"And speaking of lying in a garden," she continued,
"imagine, if you would, how soft grass can feel
against your skin on a warm spring day. It tickles a little, it cushions your body, and, if you concentrate,
you'd swear you can feel each blade pressing into you.
The smell of flowers inundates you, and the sun
warms you. You open your eyes to the bright blue,
cloudless sky, and you hear cicadas singing in the distance. That is sensuous.

"Now," Kelsey continued, "add your lover lying
there next to you, and sensuous becomes sensual…and, perhaps, sexual."

MITCH TRIED NOT TO TURN ON the radio as he drove
home. He resisted for about ninety seconds, then
flicked it on and punched the dial to Kelsey's station.
She spoke of sensuous things, and with every word,
all he could think was that her voice and her words
were the most sensuous things he'd ever experienced.
Picturing Kelsey, knowing she was saying those

words, having those thoughts and those desires, was incredibly erotic.

And incredibly frustrating.

Mitch listened the whole way home. She didn't speak all the time, breaking to play a very melodic love song, speak to one or two callers and air some commercials. But in between she continued weaving the spell of seduction that reached out through his car speakers and held him enthralled. Her entire topic tonight was on the sensuous. But she never even touched on the sensuality of a beautiful woman talking about pleasures and fulfillment, and what words and subtle nuances in a voice could do to a man.

When he reached home, Mitch hesitated before switching off the car. Leaning back in his seat, he closed his eyes, listening, savoring what she said.

"So, my friends, let me just take one more moment before we go to this next brief interruption, and make a suggestion. The next time you and your love are in an intimate moment, remember to pamper your senses. Savor the textures, and the smells, and the lovely sights. Don't rush through the sensual, savor it. This is Lady Love, and I'll be back with more music, perhaps a little poetry and more of your calls right after these messages."

Mitch turned the key and sat in the car in the darkness for a few moments. Lady Love. If he didn't know who she was, he would probably have been one of the idiots parking outside the station to get a glimpse of her. She'd seduced him, totally and completely, and at this moment, to use Paul's expression, he ached for her.

What in the name of heaven was he going to do? The most erotic, exciting woman in Baltimore lived right in his home. She slept and moved and ate and fantasized right over his head. Men all over the city were listening to her, imagining being with her, speculating on what she looked like and whether they had a chance with her.

No one but Mitch knew the woman of their dreams was Kelsey Logan, the bane of his childhood and the cause of his recent sleepless nights. Little Kelsey of the freckles and braids, his pseudo little sister.

"Hell!"

"NIGHT, BRIAN. THANKS FOR walking me out," Kelsey said as she inserted the key into the door of her car. Someone always walked her out at night. In fact, everybody left the building in pairs after dark. As Mitch had said, the station wasn't in the best part of town. But, so far, she'd never had any trouble.

"No problem, Kelsey. By the way, tonight's show was fantastic. You had 'em eating right out of your hand."

"I think we're going to have to do this topic again, soon," she said. "I was amazed at how into it some of those callers got."

Brian blew her a kiss as she waved and drove away. Kelsey knew a lot of the success of *Night Whispers* was due to Brian's hard work. She still thanked her lucky stars that Mafia Don hadn't protested too loudly when she'd coaxed Brian into following her to her new time slot. Don was one of those macho guys whose masculinity was threatened around gay men, though he'd never admit it.

She arrived home within twenty minutes and let herself into the brownstone. Locking the door behind her, Kelsey felt her way to the oak-trimmed banister. It wasn't pitch-black in the house, but the high arched window over the front door did not let in much light from the outside streetlamp.

When a shadow on the bottom of the stairs moved, she let out a small scream. Strong hands grabbed her shoulders, and a voice said, "It's me, Kelsey."

Kelsey drew a shaking hand to her heart. "Mitch, what are you doing? You scared the living daylights out of me! Why are you lurking at the bottom of the stairs in the middle of the night?"

"I couldn't sleep." His voice was steady, emotionless.

Kelsey's breathing gradually returned to normal, though adrenaline still made her pulse race. She could feel Mitch, could sense him. The hairs on her body stood up with a life of their own in an almost electric reaction to his nearness. But her eyes hadn't adjusted to the darkness, and she could barely see him.

"I was up listening to the most interesting radio program until two o'clock," he said after a moment's hesitation.

Kelsey flinched. Mitch had heard the show.

"Well, what'd you think?" she replied, forcing a bravado that she didn't feel into her tired voice.

"I'm sure you know very well what I thought, Kelsey."

"Gee, you really loved it, huh?"

"No," he replied in a sarcastic whisper. "I thought the same thing your parents would have thought—this cannot be Kelsey Logan. Kelsey Logan would not get on a public station and talk like some porn movie star."

She gasped. "That's out of line, Mitch Wymore. Way out of line, even for you."

"Is it? That's what you sounded like. Some kind of self-appointed love goddess bestowing her sexual wisdom on us mortals."

Kelsey gritted her teeth, determined not to have this argument, even though she'd actually been expecting it. "You know what? I'm not going to have this discussion with you. It's the middle of the night, and I'm tired," Kelsey said as she tried to push by him and go up the stairs.

He reached out to grab her arm as she passed. "You're not going to gloss over this, Kelsey. Does your family have any idea what you're doing? What do you think they'd say about you becoming some publicity-seeking sex goddess?"

Kelsey stopped with her hand on the banister, turned and, as her eyes were becoming accustomed to the dark, leaned until she was scant inches away from Mitch's face. "Just who do you think you are? When were you appointed to the Baltimore morality police?"

"Look, Kelsey, you're attracting the worst kind of attention. There are a lot of wackos out there who would just love to get Lady Love alone and force her to put her body where her mouth is."

She gritted her teeth, determined to remain calm and not throw a hissy fit on the stairs in the middle of the night. "Back off, Mitch. Your college professor past is showing. God, is there anyone more sanctimonious than a reformed tough guy?"

He didn't so much as grin. He obviously was not going to be teased out of his anger. "Kelsey, this just is not you."

"How would you know? You don't know me. You know nothing about the Kelsey Logan standing here with you right now. You see me as some pigtailed little kid who needs looking after, but you know what? I'm all grown-up, Mitch. And what I do is none of your business."

Kelsey tried to squeeze past Mitch and move up the stairs, to no avail. He was right in her way, and he wasn't budging. He grabbed her shoulders and forced her to stand where she was.

"I know enough about you to know that you've got a hell of a lot of talent. You could do a lot better than just titillating the public with some sordid little talk show."

Kelsey drew up a fist and punched against Mitch's chest. A cinder block might have felt softer against her fist, and she winced as pain shot up her arm. He didn't flinch.

"You're wrong. I'm an entertainer, Mitch, a performer. My audience responds to me because they like me." Kelsey suddenly wanted him to understand in spite of the fact that she really shouldn't have to explain herself to him. "And I do make them laugh. It's not always like it was tonight. Sometimes it's all lighthearted and fun, and I do wacky voices, and it's very innocent."

Mitch didn't release his grip on her shoulders, and she could see through the shadows that his stiff jaw had not relaxed one bit. He would never understand this. She could waste her breath from now until the end of the new millennium, and he'd still disapprove.

"Look, Mitch, you are *not* my brother, nor my father. You are nothing to me...." Kelsey stammered. "Nothing except my landlord, and the subject of some amusing childhood memories. So mind your own business and let me go!"

Kelsey ended on a shout, and Mitch gritted his teeth to avoid shouting right back. *Nothing?* He'd watched this stubborn, willful female grow up, had put up with years of abuse, longer years of her schoolgirl crush, and yet he was *nothing* to her? Her body shook beneath his fingers, her anger as obvious as his own.

Her husky voice echoed in his ears, and the smell of her filled his senses. Her chest heaved with her deep breaths. Her full lips were parted and she looked as if she was about to say something else. Mitch really didn't want to hear it. He just wanted her to shut up.

He had to kiss her.

Bending swiftly, he captured her open mouth with his own. She moaned, a wild sound from somewhere deep in her throat, and he pressed harder, urging her lips farther apart and sweeping his tongue against hers. She hesitated for not more than a second, then he felt her arms circle his neck as she pulled him hard against her body. Her sweet mouth welcomed him, beckoned him as he tasted her.

Kissing Kelsey was sweet and agonizing and arousing and fulfilling, all at the same time. Mitch moved his hands up her neck and cupped her face, stroking her temples and letting his fingers tangle in her loose hair. He felt her hands press into his back, pulling his body against hers. She fit against him as he'd imagined she would, as if they were made for each other.

Kelsey clung to Mitch like a drowning woman to a life raft. He filled her senses—his smell, the feel of him. In his arms, with his hot mouth on her own, she could admit that when she'd spoken of sensuous pleasures, the most rapturous one she could have imagined was the feel of this man's kiss.

And then he pulled away.

There was cold where there had been warmth. A chill touched her face and Kelsey shivered. She reached for him, wanting to draw him back, but he jerked away from her touch as if she burned him.

"I'm sorry, that should never have happened," Mitch insisted. "I was angry, and wanted to shut you up."

"It's all right," Kelsey replied, still adrift in sensation. "You didn't do anything I haven't been wanting you to do."

She smiled at him and raised a shaky finger, intending to trace the outline of his lips. He grabbed her hand, stopping her before she could touch him, and gripped it tightly.

"No, Kelsey, this was a mistake. We were both angry. It won't happen again."

He didn't want her. She bit her lip, watching the self-recrimination cross his features. He already regretted kissing her. She knew he'd been as affected by the kiss as she had, but for some reason, Mitch was not about to admit it.

"I shouldn't have ambushed you like this." He raked his hands through his hair in angry, jerky movements. "I should have waited and spoken to you in the morning, when we could both be rational about it. Let's do that, all right? We'll talk tomorrow."

He was talking about the show again, she could tell, and Kelsey's stomach tightened into a hard knot. "No, Mitch, we won't talk tomorrow. There's nothing to talk about."

"I mean," he explained, "we'll talk about the show, not about…well, what just happened."

"I know exactly what you meant." Kelsey crossed her arms firmly in front of her chest. "And, as I said, we have nothing further to discuss. It's none of your business what I do for a living. I am perfectly capable of taking care of myself. So I'll thank you to back off."

"Oh, right," he said, his voice silky and dangerous. "Like you took care of yourself a minute ago when I kissed you? You didn't fight too hard, Kelsey. What if I'd been one of Lady Love's overamorous fans?"

Kelsey narrowed her eyes and leaned forward to whisper, "Then you'd be bent over, talking in a real high-pitched voice right about now."

A light flicked on upstairs, and Kelsey jerked her head at the sound of footsteps. Fred and Celia's anxious faces peered over the rail, and she realized they must have woken them with their shouting.

"Is everything all right?" Fred asked.

"Everything's fine," Kelsey replied. "Mitch and I were just saying good-night." She stared coldly at him. "Good night, Mitch."

Not waiting for his response, Kelsey rushed up the stairs. Her feet hadn't hit the top step when she heard his door slam shut below. Tears pricked the corners of her eyes, and for the life of her she could not make her key fit into the lock.

Kelsey heard Celia's and Fred's low voices. She didn't protest when Celia approached, gently took the keys out of her hand, opened the door and led her inside.

"Thank you," she said, as Celia steered her toward her own sofa.

"No problem, honey, you look upset. Let me make you some tea to calm you down."

"I'm all right," Kelsey insisted, "though I'm about ready to strangle one overbearing anthropologist!"

Celia smoothed back Kelsey's hair and then handed

her a tissue. Fred's girlfriend looked like a little wren, with an incredibly expressive face dominated by huge brown eyes and a gentle smile. Kelsey could never imagine her raising her voice, much less screeching at a man loud enough to wake the upstairs neighbors in the middle of the night.

"I'm sorry about this, Celia. I can't believe we woke you up."

Celia filled a kettle with water and placed it on the stove. "It's all right. Though I'm sure Fred's going to turn five shades of red the next time he sees you because you and Mitch now know that I slept over."

Kelsey laughed softly, her bad mood quickly evaporating with Celia's rueful smile. "Oh, right, we never suspected. It's not as though I can see your car parked across the street when I get home at three o'clock or anything."

"I won't bother trying to hide it anymore, then," Celia said with a grin. "So, do you want to talk about...anything?"

She didn't, really. What was there to talk about? She knew from the moment she took the job at the station that Mitch and her family would never approve. His reaction tonight had come as absolutely no surprise.

"It was just a typical argument. Mitch heard my show for the first time tonight. He wasn't pleased," Kelsey admitted as she curled up in one corner of the sofa.

"I could tell," Celia said nodding slowly. "From what Fred tells me, you and he have a sort of love-hate relationship?"

"I guess you could say that." Kelsey kicked off her shoes and tucked her feet beneath her. "Mitch and I have always gotten under each other's skin. I was a pretty rotten kid, and he was the target of a lot of my pranks. Not that he was much better. He was hell on wheels himself."

"Mitch? Our Mitch?"

Kelsey grinned at the disbelief in Celia's voice. "Yes, nice, dependable, studious Mitch. He was a regular juvenile delinquent. He didn't really straighten up until he was about seventeen."

"I can't believe it. I mean, I don't know him that well, but from what Fred has said, Mitch seems almost…"

"Conservative? Don't let the brains fool you. He's somehow managed to keep his emotions suppressed, but I imagine they're still churning away somewhere deep inside. He just needs someone to remind him they're there."

"Volunteering?"

Celia laughed, but Kelsey didn't join in. "Maybe that's not such a bad idea." A slow smile spread across her lips.

"I recognize that look. That's a Lady Love face. Let me guess, you feel anything but sisterly toward him, right?" Celia asked as she carried two cups from the kitchen.

Kelsey sighed deeply. "Celia, I have been incredibly attracted to that man for years. And now, finally, I know he feels the same way. But when he allows himself to give in to those feelings for a moment, he yanks away as if he's committed some crime."

Celia didn't respond. Kelsey almost regretted taking her into her confidence. She'd never told anyone that she had the slightest interest in Mitch. It had been her secret, a schoolgirl fantasy, for many years. It was the dream she would indulge in while drying her hair or, lately, while bathing. Now that she'd said the words out loud, it was too real.

"You didn't see the way he looked at you when you stormed up the stairs," Celia said with a gentle smile. "I thought for a second he was going to grab you and throw you over his shoulder and carry you off or something...it was terribly romantic."

Kelsey gave her a sour look and stirred her tea. "If Mitch wanted to throw me anywhere, it wouldn't be over his shoulder...it would be off a bridge."

Celia sipped her tea silently. She looked like a Cheshire cat, full of secrets, sure of what she knew, and Kelsey couldn't resist asking, "You really mean it? About carrying me off, I mean?"

"He looked like a man in pain, Kelsey."

Kelsey couldn't stop the little stab of malicious pleasure that thought gave her. There had been plenty of girlish nights when she'd cried into her pillow because Mitch had called her "little brat" or given her noogies on her head.

"I think the problem is that Mitch is too decent a guy," Celia continued. "He's protective of you, wants to keep you safe from the big bad boys who might take advantage of you. And what he's feeling for you now, well, suddenly he's found out maybe he's still one of the big bad boys."

Kelsey nodded ruefully. Celia wasn't saying anything she didn't already know. Mitch was never going to willingly get involved with her. He was too honorable, too loyal to her parents. He'd accepted the "big brother" mantle her family had thrust on him and would likely never let himself touch her again. Unless...

"Celia, I've always meant to ask you. How did you ever get Fred to ask you out? The man is so shy."

"Simple," Celia answered with a smirk. "Every time I saw him, I flirted, teased and seduced him without ever letting him know I was doing it."

"Seduction, hmm? Gee, seems to me I've heard a few things about seduction."

Celia's eyes lit up as she caught Kelsey's drift. She nodded, a speculative look in her eye.

Kelsey propped her feet up on the coffee table, patting the vacant seat next to her on the sofa so Celia would sit next to her. "Tell me more."

And Celia did.

5

SOMEONE WAS POUNDING.

Kelsey buried her head under her pillow, but it did not block out the noise. She rolled over, groaning in frustration. Opening one bleary eye, she glanced at the clock. It was nearly nine.

The pounding continued. As she came more fully awake, Kelsey realized the noise wasn't coming from next door, or the street. It was coming from her front door. It had to be Mitch. Kelsey rolled out of bed, grabbed her robe and staggered out of her bedroom.

"Do you know what time it is?" she snarled as she yanked the door open.

"Good morning to you, too," Mitch said as he breezed past her into her apartment. "Like bagels?"

He looked bright and chipper and Kelsey really wanted to sock him one. "You know I hate bagels."

"I know. That's why I brought doughnuts," he said as he made himself at home at her small café-style kitchen table and tore open the bag. Her efficiency kitchen was really not much larger than a closet, and flowed right into the living area. Kelsey had placed the table and chairs as a sort of divider, and his large form dominated the small space.

"What do you want?" she grumbled.

"Coffee would be nice. Or even milk."

She knew full well he was stalling. "I mean, why are you here?"

"I think we need to talk," he replied. "I did a lot of thinking last night."

"Then how come you're up so early?" she asked, shooting him a glare from behind lowered lids. Kelsey plopped onto the sofa, leaned her head back and closed her eyes.

"I never need more than six or seven hours of sleep. Don't you remember?"

Of course she remembered. When they were kids, Mitch had always been the first one awake in the house, which had driven her right up the wall on many Saturday mornings when she'd come downstairs to watch *Land of the Lost* and he'd already been engrossed in *Johnny Quest*.

"Right. Mr. Perfect. Now, what do you want?"

Kelsey realized she wasn't being friendly. So much for her conversation with Celia about how to attract or, more accurately, seduce, Mitch. Right now she just wanted to shove him back down the stairs, get a little more sleep and face him later in the day, after she'd at least had a chance to brush her teeth.

"I came to apologize."

Kelsey opened her eyes and sat up straight. "So…apologize."

"I'm trying to," Mitch said ruefully. "It's not easy."

"I'm sure you're not in the habit of having to admit you were wrong."

Mitch helped himself to a powdered sugar doughnut. "That's not why I'm having a problem. I wasn't wrong. I still believe everything I said to you last night. I'm just apologizing for ambushing you and for taking advantage of the situation."

"You mean kissing me?"

"Yeah. Kissing you. It was out of line."

"Right," she said in a steely tone. "Kissing me was a crime against the nation. Are you finished?"

Mitch could tell Kelsey was getting upset as she leaned forward and started tapping her fingers on her knee. She wore her little green robe and looked all rumpled, with her hair puffy and wild, and no makeup. Mitch knew if he closed his eyes he would imagine her lying in her bed, without the robe, beckoning to him.

He forced himself to stop his wandering thoughts. Taking a big bite out of the messy doughnut, he glanced around for a napkin to stall for time.

He was going about this all wrong. His plan was to come up and smooth things over, to start their conversation again, and to try to talk some sense into her. Instead he found himself hip deep in the topic he most wanted to avoid: their kiss. Thinking of that kiss, and of her all sleepy and seductive, had already caused him enough trouble. After he had gotten over his anger at their argument, he'd been able to think of nothing else the previous night.

Mitch had never imagined that one kiss, a first kiss, could start such a flame. He'd burned. Long after she went upstairs, he'd sat in his apartment and done a slow, agonizing burn for her. But he'd mentally doused that fire and decided on a course of action. He would go right back to treating Kelsey like a kid sister, and would never let on that the kiss meant a thing. He'd ignore the fact that he got hard just remembering it.

"Look, let's chalk it up to the heat of the moment and forget about it, okay?" He tried very hard to keep his voice steady and noncommittal. "It was a kiss. Big deal."

To Kelsey, it *had* been a big deal. But Mitch obviously didn't view it the same way. Kelsey wished she was still in bed and this was all a dream. The day was going from bad to worse, and she'd only been awake for five minutes. Having Mitch angry at himself for kissing her had been bad enough. But having him blow off the whole event as no big deal just plain hurt.

"Fine. Right," she replied, determined not to let him see how his words affected her. "As the song goes... 'a kiss is just a kiss.' And, hey, look who you're talking to... Lady Love. I should know."

Mitch's jaw stiffened. "You wanna explain that?"

"No, Mitch. As I told you last night, I don't have to explain a thing to you," Kelsey said. "I am an adult. You are an adult. We happen to live in the same building. What I do for a living has nothing to do with you."

Mitch nodded slowly. "I know."

Kelsey ran a weary hand over her eyes, trying to follow his logic. "You know? Then why are you here?"

"Just because I know you're right that it's none of my business doesn't mean I like it, or that I won't try to talk you out of it, Kelsey. It simply means I acknowledge the fact that my opinion really doesn't matter to you."

Mitch wouldn't meet her eye, and Kelsey felt a moment's remorse for some of the things she'd said to him the night before. Mitch did matter... she was beginning to suspect he mattered too much!

"That's not true. Mitch, I respect you. I think you're a very intelligent man and I value your opinion. But, in this case, I don't know that you've formed your thoughts rationally. You heard one show. Give me a chance, please. Listen in a few more times. The show is not what you think it is."

"And if I listen, and my views don't change?" he asked, arching an eyebrow at her as he waited for her reply.

"I don't know, Mitch," she said, eyes flashing as she stood and walked toward him. "I guess if your views don't change, you have the right to turn the radio off and pretend I'm the weather girl. I'm not going to tell you I'll quit my job because you don't like it."

Her robe swished around her body as she walked. He couldn't stop staring at the peach flesh of her upper leg, exposed as her robe gapped with each step. She reached the table and stopped right next to him.

"So what you're telling me," he replied slowly as he let his gaze burn a path up her thigh, across her body and up to her face, "is that I should give you another chance, listen more, and maybe I'll like what I hear, but if I don't, then I should go take a flying leap. Do I have this right?"

Kelsey grabbed a glazed doughnut, held it speculatively in front of her face, then looked down to stare at him.

"Yeah, I guess you do."

Mitch stood very slowly. She had come to stand close to him, nearly between his legs, and he did a slow slide up her body, feeling a crackle of electricity flash in the scant inch that separated them. She had to tilt her head back to maintain their eye contact, and Mitch suddenly had the advantage.

"Kelsey?" he said softly, a dangerous gleam in his eyes.

She backed up a tiny step. He followed until again they were nearly touching.

"What?"

"To hell with that," he retorted.

Kelsey watched Mitch drop the half-eaten doughnut on the table, turn and stride out the door.

"Well," she muttered after he'd gone, "so much for seduction!"

LATER THAT DAY, after Kelsey had managed another hour of fitful sleep, she went downstairs, carrying a paperback and a tall glass of iced tea. It was still relatively warm for mid-October, and she meant to enjoy the weather while it lasted. Not wanting to risk another confrontation with Mitch, she was quiet as she slipped through the kitchen to the back door.

Slight hints of yellow tinged leaves on the trees. A smoky smell hung in the air, and Kelsey knew someone was anticipating the cold weather with an early season fire. Dragging a lawn chair from the garage, she placed it under a tall shady maple in the backyard. Her long-sleeved cotton shirt and khaki pants were perfectly adequate for warmth. Kelsey breathed deeply, invigorated by the clean, crisp breeze. She would lie here and read her romance novel and not think at all about Mitch.

But she couldn't even open the book. She kept staring at the picture on the cover. The hero was gorgeous, larger than life, but he still wasn't as handsome as her frustrating landlord. As for the heroine...well, Kelsey figured she'd have a really tough time buying blouses that fit.

"Shall we try this again?" came a familiar drawl.

Kelsey jerked her head and dropped the book at the

sound of Mitch's voice. He stood right beside her. She hadn't even detected his approach.

"You're quiet as a cat," she said. "That's the second time you've done that to me."

Kelsey watched as Mitch leaned back against the maple tree and stared down at her. Taking a few deep breaths, she tried to slow her rapid pulse. She would play this cool if it killed her. What had Celia said? Flirt, seduce, all without his knowledge. She could do that. After all, she was Lady Love. Kelsey felt like a soap opera diva at the thought.

"Look, we live under the same roof, whether I like it or not," he finally said. "And we have to find a way to get along."

"We already do get along, Mitch. I really don't see the problem."

"Right. Yeah, well, that's what I came out to say. There's really no problem. As you said, I'm merely your landlord, of absolutely no importance in your life. That fact has finally sunk in. You do your thing, Kelsey, and I'll mind my own business. And as you also said last night, I'm really nothing to you. We'll be acquaintances who nod at each other on the stairs, all right?"

No. No, that was not all right. Acquaintances? How could he say that? Even if Kelsey had never laid eyes on Mitch until she moved to the city, if their childhood lives had never collided, she still felt they were a heck of a long way from mere "acquaintances." However, since she'd said much the same thing during their dispute, she couldn't very well disagree with him now. She wished she'd refrained from arguing with him and just continued up the stairs when she'd gotten home last night. But then, if she'd done that, they would never have shared that kiss. And she knew down to her very soul that she would never regret finally being in Mitch's arms.

"Please, don't get the wrong idea," she said, "I really didn't mean to offend you earlier. I care what you think, I really do."

Mitch shrugged. "It doesn't matter. As far as I'm concerned, it's finished."

Kelsey watched him turn to leave. Mitch was in such a strange mood, so somber and unemotional. In all the years she'd known him, she had never seen him so…remote.

"I've gotta go," he said as he walked away.

Mitch managed to reach the house without turning back to look at Kelsey one more time. He refused to let her see that their conversation bothered him in the least. She'd looked so lovely, with a few loose tendrils of hair blowing free, and her angelic face turned toward the sun. But he had to stop thinking of her in that way. There were plenty of beautiful women in Baltimore. As far as he was concerned, Kelsey barely even existed anymore.

Mitch had spent a good bit of the morning racking his brain over their fight and hadn't been any closer to a solution when he'd received a call an hour ago. Kelsey's mother wanted to welcome Mitch home, and to sincerely thank him for "taking care" of Kelsey. She assured him again that she and Ralph were so happy Kelsey had a "member of the family" to look after her in Baltimore.

Fifteen minutes later, Nathan called and he heard the entire speech over again. Mitch was tempted to tell her brother that while Kelsey might seem a fairly inexperienced young woman, her alternate persona,

Lady Love, seemed an expert. Instead, he'd kept Kelsey's secret and assured Nathan that she would be as safe in his house as she'd been at home. That meant safe from everyone. Including himself. So it was time to draw the line and stay well behind it.

Mitch still believed this solution was for the best. He'd already allowed Kelsey to creep into his life and it was time to put a stop to it. If she wanted to go on the radio and titillate the entire city, she was welcome to do it. He didn't have to think about it, absolutely was not going to listen, and they certainly didn't have to socialize. There should be no reason why they should have more than minimal contact. And that was fine with him.

"NOT ON YOUR LIFE, Mitch Wymore," Kelsey whispered as she watched Mitch enter the house. "You are not going to shut me out."

Mitch wanted to pretend they meant nothing to each other. Well, he could pretend all he wanted to. But he wouldn't get away with it. They lived in the same house, parked their cars two feet away from one another, bumped into each other at the mailbox, or while getting the newspaper. No way was he going to be able to avoid her.

She would make sure of that.

"LET'S TALK ABOUT DESIRE."

Kelsey sat in her studio, opening her show even before the last notes of her introduction were finished. She was more than prepared for tonight's topic.

"Now I don't mean the natural urge we have to be close to someone we love, to further our deep emotions for that person through physical expression.

That's wonderful, too, of course. But tonight, I want to talk about the kind of desire that's almost painful in its intensity. You know what I mean...the sweaty palms, the pounding heart, the tense, coiled feeling in the pit of your stomach when you think of someone you want so badly but haven't been with. Think about it. You know what I'm talking about. Stick around. It should be an interesting night."

Kelsey sat back during her first set of commercials, winking at Brian while she sipped a glass of water. Usually she kept her personal feelings out of her show. She considered Lady Love to be a character she portrayed. But after days of doing her best to make Mitch want her, she was very much acquainted with wanting someone and was quite ready to talk about unfulfilled desire.

When Brian cued her, she leaned forward and said, "Welcome back to *Night Whispers* on WAJO. I'm Lady Love and tonight we're going to explore that intoxicating feeling of just *wanting* someone. Let's not muddy the waters, we're not talking about lifelong love. When you find your one and only, the desire changes, it becomes more meaningful, more fulfilling. That's another topic for another show. Instead, let's focus on that spine-tingling sensation you get when you're around someone who you just *know* could give you immense physical pleasure."

Sultry images flooded her mind, but Kelsey forced herself to keep focused on what she was doing.

"Have you felt it? Do you feel it now?" she asked, her voice challenging her listeners. "Can you close your eyes and picture every inch of the person you want?"

She had. She did. She could.

"Sometimes the person we want isn't right for us, or doesn't feel the same way. But that doesn't stop the need. Pure, undiluted desire. We've all experienced it. Now let's talk about it."

"HOLY HELL!" MITCH MUTTERED. He kicked a pile of papers out of his way as he stalked across the living room and punched the off button on his stereo. Still not satisfied, he reached behind it and yanked the cord out of the wall. He didn't know what demon had made him tune in to begin with.

"Shut up, Kelsey. Just leave me alone," he muttered aloud in the empty room.

But she wouldn't. Kelsey would not leave him alone.

He glanced at the notes he'd been writing before her show came on. It wouldn't do any good to try to get back to work. Every time he tried to concentrate, thoughts of Kelsey intruded.

For the past week, while he'd struggled to avoid her, she'd turned up everywhere. When he went outside to change the oil in his car, she came out in a pair of very tight, torn jeans and a T-shirt to wash hers. The water had splashed her, making the shirt stick to her skin. He'd been paying so much attention to her that he'd forgotten what he was doing and neglected to tighten the filter. When oil came spilling out on the driveway he'd had to dive back under the car, getting his clothes black and sticky. She'd rushed over to help him clean up, dabbing at the stains while he sucked in gulps of air and tried to look everywhere but at her totally wet, nearly transparent shirt.

When he pulled a load of clothes from the dryer, he bumped into her coming up the basement stairs, and had to lift the laundry basket high over his head while she scooted past. As she slid by, he'd swear she purposely brushed her entire body against his, saying, "We're just supposed to nod, right?" He stared down at her, watching her descend, as her light, flowery scent hung in the air. She hadn't even looked back at him standing mute on the stairs.

When he went out to cut the grass, he found her pulling weeds in the garden. Yesterday, when he got home, he found her baking sweet-smelling cinnamon rolls in his kitchen. For several minutes, while he put away his groceries, he had to watch her slowly licking sticky, sweet icing from her fingers.

And all the while she smiled and batted her lashes and played the role of temptress as though she'd invented it.

"You're not going to get away with this, Kelsey," Mitch said aloud as he walked to his office and flipped on his computer.

He knew he was being played like an instrument. Kelsey was trying to make him admit they could never be mere acquaintances, or housemates. She didn't like him criticizing her job, but then, when he'd come up with an ideal solution, she didn't like that, either.

Tonight she must have suspected he'd listen to her show. She seemed to be speaking directly to him. Telling him she wanted him. He didn't know whether to be flattered or just plain frustrated.

At this particular moment, he was opting for frustrated.

LATE THE NEXT AFTERNOON, Kelsey sat with Celia in Fred's apartment, waiting for a batch of cookies to finish baking.

"How is it going with Mitch?" Celia asked.

"It's not going at all," Kelsey replied with a sigh. "He's not responding in the least. He doesn't appear to even be aware of me."

Celia grinned. "You must be joking. I was watching out the window the other day when you washed your car. He definitely knew you were there. Fred thought I was crazy for laughing when Mitch got himself covered with oil."

"Well," Kelsey conceded, "he knows I'm around, he's just not ready to admit he *cares* I'm around. I think it was better when we were just friends. This acquaintance business is getting tiresome."

"So, you just want to be friends again? Yeah, right," Celia said with a knowing smile.

"Well, maybe *friends* isn't quite the right word."

Celia crossed her arms across her chest and raised one eyebrow. "I think *lovers* is the word you're looking for."

Kelsey laughed at Celia's droll tone. "The thought has crossed my mind."

"A woman would have to be made of stone for that thought not to cross her mind when Mitch Wymore walked into a room."

Kelsey pretended she was shocked. "Why, Celia, for a nearly engaged woman to say such a thing…I'm appalled!"

"Hey, I love Fred, okay?" Celia explained with a laugh. "But that doesn't mean I can't appreciate a male body that looks like it should be a centerfold…or a face that looks like it should be on the cover of *GQ*."

"Don't forget those dark blue eyes that seem to see everything," Kelsey contributed.

"I think I prefer green eyes." Celia's sweet smile told Kelsey she had switched her thoughts to Fred.

When they heard a car pull up outside, Celia glanced out the window. "Fred's home. Looks like he's unloading some boxes. Uh-oh, Mitch is going out to help him."

"I think I'll slide on outta here, then," Kelsey said. "I'm not exactly dressed for another seduction attempt."

Kelsey glanced ruefully at her purple sweat suit and sneakers as she carried her teacup into the kitchen. She had a little flour on her chest from the cookie baking, and a brown smear on her wristband where she'd accidentally leaned into a bowl of chocolate chips.

"Don't go," Celia said. "When they get up here I'll order pizzas or something, and the four of us can have dinner."

"With Mitch ignoring me and me drooling over him? Thanks, but no thanks."

"You don't drool, and he doesn't ignore you."

"I appreciate the offer, but I am about ready to call this plan quits, anyway. Mitch has made it clear he's not interested, and I'm not about to ambush him. Besides, my producer, Brian, is stopping by later. I need to get home and make some notes about show ideas before he arrives."

Kelsey opened the apartment door to leave and found Fred, carrying a large carton, reaching for the knob. She held the door for him, and said hello and goodbye. Hoping Mitch wouldn't be too quick, she dashed to the stairs and was halfway down when he started coming up. He hadn't seen her yet; the large box he carried blocked his view. Kelsey decided to press against the wall and let him move right past her on the wide stairway. With any luck he'd never even notice she was there. It almost worked.

Mitch peered around the side of the carton he was carrying to see if he was nearing the top step, and came face-to-face with Kelsey. Startled, he dropped the box, watching helplessly as plastic beakers and papers spilled onto the wooden stairs. The cardboard container tipped on its side and slid like a toboggan straight down to the landing.

"What do you think you're doing?"

"I'm sorry, I was just trying to get out of your way." Kelsey shrugged slightly, but grimaced at the loud thump of the box hitting the floor at the bottom of the steps.

"Dammit, Kelsey," Mitch snapped as he faced her and moved closer. "This is going to stop. Understand?" Kelsey leaned back farther as he crowded her. His hands braced the wall on either side of her head, and he trapped her, inches from his chest, as he continued his tirade. "I hope Fred didn't have anything breakable in that box. What a dumb stunt!"

Mitch stared hard at her, looking for the gleam of mischief he felt sure he'd find, but it wasn't there. She looked contrite, embarrassed even. And a mess.

A smudge of flour rode the high plane of her cheek, and her hair hung in disarray from a clip. He watched her part her full lips and take in a deep breath, and noticed the strong pulse beating in her throat. She was nervous—he could see it. A slow flush spread from her neck up through her face, and her breathing became more labored. Mitch glanced down to the slight space between their bodies. Not much more than a whisper separated them.

He dropped his voice to a growl. "All right, Kelsey. You win."

Kelsey raised her eyes in confusion, but didn't have time to absorb his words when his mouth suddenly captured hers in a searing kiss. She didn't move, didn't have the strength to lift her arms to encircle his neck, but reveled in the hard press of his body, crushing hers from shoulder to thigh. His hot mouth urged hers to open and she welcomed him, loving the intimacy, the taste of him as the kiss continued endlessly.

She whimpered when Mitch moved his hands to her shoulders, then slowly slid them down her arms until he reached her fingertips. He laced his fingers through hers briefly, then moved his hands to her hips, pulling her tighter against him. Her whimper turned into a moan at the feel of his hard excitement. Mitch lifted his mouth from hers, trailing hot kisses down her chin, across her neck, to the hollow of her throat. His fingertips reached her waist and slid under her sweatshirt, caressing her sensitive, bare flesh.

Kelsey shifted a little, silently urging him to continue exploring her body, as she longed to do with his. Finally regaining the ability to move, she allowed her palms to travel up the flat expanse of his stomach to his hard chest. She stroked the side of his neck, then curled her fingers in his hair.

Mitch inhaled Kelsey's scent as he trailed kisses along her throat. He lightly grazed his teeth against the soft curve of her neck as he caressed her bare midriff, then moved his hands higher to rest just underneath her breasts.

"Oh, Mitch, yes, please," she whispered brokenly in that deep, throaty voice he knew so well.

Mitch closed his eyes tightly as her words intruded on the seductive spell he'd allowed to envelop him. Pulling his fingers away from her skin, he leaned his forehead on the wall behind her and struggled mightily to slow his rapid, shallow breathing.

After a few seconds he pulled back from her, looking at her dazed expression. Her head was thrown back, eyes closed, and deep breaths came from between her swollen lips. Desire for her rose again, almost as swiftly as his anger at his lack of control. He didn't know whether he was more angry at himself for forgetting his resolutions regarding Kelsey, or at her for being so damned tempting.

"Are you satisfied now?" he asked raggedly.

Kelsey slowly shook her head and replied without even opening her eyes, "I'm a long way from satisfied."

So was he. Mitch knew the only way he'd be satisfied right now was if he buried himself inside her body and felt her sleek legs wrapped around his waist.

"This is insane," he muttered as he angrily thrust his hands through his hair. "What are we doing?"

She smiled slowly without bothering to open her eyes. "Exactly what we've both been wanting to do, I believe."

Mitch shook his head in disbelief. She was so matter-of-fact, as if this moment of wild, unexpected passion was the most natural thing in the world. As if the two of them could forget the past, and her family, and their long-standing connection, and just drift into a reckless affair.

He stared steadily at her. "What do you want from me?"

Oh, if he only knew what she wanted! She wanted Fred and Celia to disappear. She wanted Mitch to yank her clothes off and lift her up so she could wrap her legs around him. She wanted him pressing her against the wall as he filled her body and they let the passion consume them.

And more than anything, she wanted to wake up tomorrow morning, and many mornings thereafter, and find him next to her.

"I think that if I answer that question honestly you're going to go back down to your apartment, lock your door and never come near me again," she said softly.

Mitch backed away and studied Kelsey's face. She was not flirting, she was not trying to seduce or cajole. Her honest desire was plain to see, and her bright green eyes held absolutely nothing back. All she wanted was him.

God help him, all he wanted was her, too. His blood coursed through his veins and excitement threatened to overwhelm him. For the first time in years, he felt totally in tune with his senses, remembering every soft inch of her flesh, the sweet scent of her aroused body. He wanted to take her, right there on the stairs, to hell with Fred and Celia and anybody else. But he couldn't. He couldn't say to hell with her family.

Finally, when he trusted himself to speak without telling her how much his body was screaming for her, he muttered, "Then maybe we'd better forget I asked."

6

THE ICE CUBES CLINKED against his glass as Mitch swirled his drink. He stared pensively out his front window at the night sky, wondering what kind of fool he'd been to walk away from Kelsey.

Mitch had never wanted a woman as much as he'd wanted her at that moment. He'd never been as aroused, or as totally unaware of where he was and who was present. He'd felt like a kid again, conscious of nothing but feeling, not caring about anything but physical pleasure.

He didn't know how he managed to turn his back on her and begin gathering Fred's spilled belongings. Kelsey had moved past him with quiet dignity and entered her apartment. After dumping the box unceremoniously in Fred's apartment, Mitch had gone back downstairs, resisting the strong temptation to stop at Kelsey's door, knock, and see what happened when she answered.

He did the right thing. Things had gotten a little carried away *again*, but there was no sense in making a difficult situation worse. Maybe he'd been a little crazy to think he and Kelsey could be nothing but neighbors; too many years of history made a mockery of that idea. But they could not become lovers. For about the hundredth time that evening, he found himself wishing she'd never moved in. And for about the hundredth time that evening, he called himself a liar as he remembered the feel of her pressed against him.

Mitch heard the doorbell ring. Glancing at the clock, he saw it was after nine, and knew exactly who was showing up. Kelsey's date. Celia had mentioned earlier that she'd invited Kelsey to stay for dinner but that she had other plans, with a man, for that evening.

Good. That was exactly what she should be doing. Getting out, meeting people, forgetting all about him.

"You're such a liar," Mitch said aloud, knowing he'd rather have both his legs broken than have her forget all about him. He started pouring himself another drink as he heard Kelsey come down the stairs and greet her guest. When he heard them go back upstairs to her apartment, he made it a double.

"I REALLY APPRECIATE you coming by and going over these show ideas with me, Brian. And thanks for dinner."

Kelsey sat on the floor of her apartment, leaning on her coffee table to write on a yellow legal tablet. She absently picked up her cold-cuts sub and took a bite.

"No problem," he replied. "I wasn't doing anything tonight, anyway. Chuck's working a double so I would have been sitting around at home."

"So, what's my excuse for having nothing to do and nowhere to go on a Saturday night?"

"Oh, make me laugh. Half the guys at the station would ask you out in a second if you gave the slightest indication you were interested," Brian argued as he glanced at his notebook.

"But would it be me they were asking out, or Lady Love?"

"If Lady Love were interested, you'd have half the

guys in Baltimore at your door. But from that moony look you get on your face whenever you start talking about this guy who lives downstairs, I guess Lady Love's not available."

Kelsey grimaced and wiped her sticky fingers on a napkin.

"I'm not moony," she said. She hadn't realized her feelings for Mitch had been so obvious. Of course, Brian was very perceptive.

"No, of course you're not, sweetie," Brian said with a grin, as if humoring her mood.

Her mood stank. After Mitch's rejection earlier that afternoon, she hadn't known whether to laugh or cry. She'd done a little of both, then sat quietly and calmly and thought about her relationship with Mitch.

It was done. Whatever fantasies she had about him were finished, and good riddance to them. Well, she had to admit, maybe her fantasies themselves weren't done. After that kiss, that embrace, that flash of absolute electricity they'd shared, she imagined her fantasies were going to get a lot more intense! But her slight belief that maybe something would come of those fantasies...that was gone. Mitch had rejected her for the last time. Right now, he was probably feeling so embarrassed he wouldn't come near her again. And that suited her just fine.

MITCH WASN'T THINKING totally clearly, but he knocked on her door anyway, muttering, "I owe you one, Kelsey Logan. You've got this coming."

He shivered slightly as a draft swept up from downstairs, blowing under the towel he wore around his hips. Curling his toes on the cool wood floor, he wished she'd hurry up and answer. Every second she delayed made him think about heading back downstairs. But his reflexes were perhaps the tiniest bit slower because of his mood...and, possibly, the scotch. Before he had time to forget the whole stupid idea, Kelsey's apartment door opened.

Kelsey had really expected Celia to be standing in her doorway with a plateful of cookies. Instead, a six-foot-tall, nearly naked, rock-hard, golden, lean man stood there.

"Hello, Kelsey," Mitch said with a slow smile as he sauntered into her apartment. "Gee, seems I'm all out of soap. Got some I could borrow?"

Kelsey stared as Mitch moved past her. He was naked. Well, not entirely, she supposed. He wore a white towel around his waist, but otherwise, nothing. His dark hair was mussed, damp, as if he had just jumped in the shower, then jumped back out. A drop of water fell from one lock of hair and landed on his sculpted bronzed shoulder, slowly gliding a glistening path down the crisp, dark hair on his chest. She followed the droplet's descent, and then allowed her eyes to travel farther down his body. A quivering sigh was the only sound she could manage.

Kelsey had a pretty good idea what men were supposed to look like. She'd been raised with two brothers, after all, and had enjoyed her fair share of male attention. But Mitch, well, she'd never seen a man who made her forget to breathe.

He was beautiful. His body was hard but not bulky. Lean, toned, with sinewy muscles that rippled along his chest and upper arms. His flesh was smooth, unmarred, a delicious light tan color. Her mouth suddenly felt very dry. The dark hair on his chest was sparse and tapered to a thin line down his flat stomach. The white towel interrupted her gaze, but she skimmed it and studied his firm legs. Even his feet were sexy.

Kelsey felt like one of those gaping, foolish men so often seen in comedy movies, ogling a gorgeous woman in a bikini. She quickly glanced up to see if Mitch had noticed.

He smirked.

"Ah-hem," a voice intruded. Mitch glanced nonchalantly over his shoulder to the dark-haired man standing near the sofa. "Oh, I'm sorry, do you have company?" he drawled.

"I was just leaving," the other man said. He eyed Mitch from head to toe, then glanced at Kelsey and gave her a huge grin and a wink. Mitch couldn't understand why Kelsey's date would be so amused at another man, nearly naked, bursting in on them, and why he would cut and run at the sight of the competition. But he really didn't care. The guy was leaving. More important, he and Kelsey had both been fully clothed, sitting in the living room, when Mitch arrived!

Kelsey found her vocal cords and managed to say, "Uh, yeah, thanks, Brian."

Brian surreptitiously gave her a thumbs-up as Kelsey returned his quick kiss on the cheek. Her producer looked highly amused, and she imagined she'd have a lot of explaining to do Monday night.

"Gee, don't run off on my account. I really didn't mean to interrupt your date," Mitch said with an absolute lack of sincerity.

"No problem," Brian responded as he stood by the open door. "Kelsey's not my type, anyway."

Mitch shrugged as the other man gave him another

long glance, then sighed and slipped out the door. Suddenly he noticed Kelsey beginning to chuckle. He turned to face her as her chuckles turned to uproarious, gut-clenching laughter, and she fell to the couch.

"What's so funny?" he asked indignantly.

Kelsey couldn't answer him. Oh, it was too much! Mitch was paying her back for the trick she'd played on him with that blond witch. He thought Brian was her date, and he'd come up here to give her a little taste of her own medicine.

Finally, she calmed down and looked over to where Mitch stood, looking at her as if she were insane.

"I'm sorry," she said between giggles. "It's just…well, if Brian were to come to the brownstone for a date, I imagine he'd be knocking on your door…or Fred's."

Mitch didn't understand for a moment. Then it sank in. Kelsey's "date" was gay. Mitch tried for self-righteous indignation. He tried to be offended. He tried to feel stupid that his plan had blown up in his slightly drunk face. But he couldn't. He started laughing and fell to the couch to sit beside Kelsey, who once again erupted in chuckles.

When they'd both calmed down, Kelsey said, "Oh, Mitch, what were you thinking? What would possess you to come up here like this?"

"Like this?" Mitch asked as he playfully stood and posed in the towel.

She grinned at his impersonation of a muscle-man, not that he couldn't pull it off, but because she knew him so well. Mitch had never flaunted his looks. His personality and brains had taken him anywhere he ever wanted to go. But, oh, if ever a man was born who could have coasted a little on an absolutely mouthwatering physique, this was he.

"Well," he continued, "I suppose I could have come like...this."

Mitch grabbed the knot at his hip and loosened it, giving her an evil leer. Kelsey gasped and threw her hands over her eyes, but peeked through her fingers as the towel dropped to the floor.

"You cheater," she exclaimed when she saw the running shorts he was wearing.

He grinned wickedly. "Did you think I'd be crazy enough to come up here totally naked under that towel?"

"I don't know," she replied. "When you were a kid you might have. But the Mitch Wymore I've been sharing this house with for the past few weeks...he's so uptight, I'm surprised he didn't show up in a three-piece suit."

"Uptight?" he exclaimed with mock offense. "I am the least uptight person on the planet. Unless, of course, you happen to be Lady Love, the sex queen of Baltimore."

Kelsey searched his face for any bitterness but saw only his teasing laughter. "I miss you, Mitch. I miss this. I miss my friend."

"Kels, we've never really been friends. You were a royal pain in the butt."

"Speak for yourself," she said as she swatted at him with a pillow. "Seriously, do you think we could manage friendship? I mean, acquaintances, that's absolutely out. And you've made it perfectly clear you don't want anything more...intimate. Can we just be friends?"

Kelsey sounded uncertain, her voice quivered.

Could it be she didn't know how much he desired her? Could she really not tell that this whole fiasco tonight had been prompted by pure jealousy?

Mitch didn't question her. Kelsey was giving him exactly what he wanted, what was right. Friendship with no strings. Perfect. He would forget about desire. He hoped.

"Being friends sounds great, Kelsey."

AT TEN O'CLOCK THE NEXT MORNING, Kelsey stood outside the door to Mitch's apartment and knocked sharply. He'd asked her to come down and help him sort some paperwork in the spirit of their new friendship.

"Reporting for duty, sir," she said as Mitch answered his door.

"Come on in," he replied.

Kelsey entered Mitch's apartment, noting the piles of papers and pictures on every available surface. She didn't bother to ask why they weren't working in his office; she'd cleaned in there a few times while he was gone and, if anything, that room was even worse.

"What do you need me to do?"

"Actually, I really need help putting this stuff in some kind of order. I had several rolls of film developed, and I've listed the subjects in my journals. Could you match the rolls with the notes? It would be a big help."

Kelsey sat on the sofa and picked up a packet of pictures. "I can do that. Are these pictures going to be in the book?"

He wryly shook his head. "No way. This is a collaborative effort. The publisher has professional photographers, graphic artists, even other writers for certain sections. These are just for my notes…and my memories."

Mitch surreptitiously watched Kelsey work. Her tawny hair swung forward, covering her cheek, and he took advantage of the moment to drink her in with his eyes. This "friends" thing was playing havoc with his peace of mind. He grinned, teased, talked about his trip and answered her endless questions, carefully hiding the fact that he wanted to strip off her fluffy sweater and lick her collarbone.

"Who are these children?" she asked.

Glad she'd distracted him from his wandering thoughts, Mitch glanced at the photos she held. Gazing at the eager faces, he smiled. "These are China's little angels. They're the unwanted ones. The baby girls who've been abandoned and are raised in state homes."

Mitch saw a frown cross her face. Her shoulders drooped as she sat cross-legged on the floor, next to the sofa.

"Oh, of course, I remember reading your articles in the Baltimore paper a few months ago. These are the girls who are suffering because of China's one-child policy. Now I understand why there are no boys," she said softly.

"You don't usually see boys in these places unless they're ill or handicapped." Mitch set the pictures on the table. "Boys are a valuable commodity in a land where parents are punished for having more than one child. If a couple has no son, there's no one to support them in their old age. Baby girls are found abandoned every day, and they're usually taken directly to an orphanage. Officials seldom even try to find out who they belong to."

"How could parents do that to a child?" Kelsey asked in dismay.

"Chinese parents love their children as much as we do, Kels. They're in an untenable situation, and are forced to do something morally repugnant to survive. I'm sure most Chinese mothers mourn the loss of their daughters all their lives."

Kelsey stared at the pictures on the table, captivated by the faces, the bright-eyed optimism of the beautiful little girls.

"Your articles helped them, you know," she said softly. "I read that there has been a recent surge in foreign adoptions."

He nodded. "That makes it worthwhile. Believe it or not, I even thought about it myself while I was there. For the first time in my life I thought long and hard about becoming a father, even though I'd never believed that would happen."

Kelsey quickly looked up at him. "Why not? I'm sure you'd be a great father. What kid wouldn't want a dad who knows how to hot-wire a car?"

He shook his head, chuckling, and replied, "I've come a long way from those days. It's funny when you think about it. I grew up resentful as hell toward my parents, and ended up a lot like them...a little introverted, a little selfish. I travel all the time. I'm not cut out for home, family and kids. The only times I ever felt a family connection were when I was staying with your parents."

She gave him a sour look. "You sure were around enough to be a Logan!"

"To me, you were like a television show from the fifties that I could step into and pretend I was part of for a little while. But I never felt I was really one of you."

She stared at him, knowing what he said was true. Mitch had always been a little removed from them, always prepared for the rug to be pulled out from under him. At first it was evident in his rebellion, later in his self-imposed isolation.

"Anyway," he continued, "I'm not really cut out for kids, just as my parents weren't."

"I'm quite sure your parents love you, Mitch. But admit it, you weren't the easiest kid to deal with."

She saw his wicked grin and knew he was indulging in a little reminiscing about his hellion years.

"I know you're right," he said. "I was totally out of their realm. I got more interesting to them when I was older, once your parents helped me overcome my tendency toward self-destruction. And they're certainly pleased I ended up so *respectable*."

He said the word as if it pained him, and Kelsey grinned. "I somehow suspect they know you well enough to be aware that the badass in you is always lurking just underneath the surface."

He shook his head ruefully, leaned back on the sofa and said, "Kelsey, until you moved into my life, I would have sworn that *badass* was long gone!"

"Gee, that's the nicest thing you've ever said to me, Mitch," she said with a self-satisfied smirk.

"Don't let it go to your head."

Kelsey slid up on the sofa to sit next to him. Papers and books covered two of the three cushions, and Kelsey nudged Mitch with her hip until he made room for her. He gave a loud, theatrical sigh as she sat down.

"Admit it, I'm not so bad to have around."

He glanced at her out of the corner of his eye.

"There are a few definite benefits to having you around, Kels."

She liked the sound of that.

"Mainly, it earns me points with your family."

She elbowed him in the ribs. "Not funny."

Kelsey reached out to retrieve the stack of pictures on the table, slowly flipping through them again. She sensed Mitch watching her. His body was pressed against hers, from hip to knee. When he stretched his arm across the back of the sofa behind her, she curled up into the crook under his arm. He didn't pull away. Kelsey closed her eyes briefly and savored the heavy weight of his arm on her shoulders, and the faint scent of his cologne. His neck was inches from her face, and the urge to press a kiss below his right ear was nearly overwhelming. She resisted it by focusing on the pictures. He took a few from her and glanced through them himself.

"You're wrong, you know," she said as they finished going through the stack. "You have a huge heart, Mitch. You are not destined to be alone."

She turned her face up to look at him, staring intently into his dark blue eyes. He didn't say anything. Kelsey couldn't stop looking at him, knowing she wasn't quite staying within the "friends" boundary they'd decided on. She didn't care. She'd be willing to bet money that he didn't, either. Especially when she realized he was going to kiss her.

He leaned forward slowly and brought his lips to hers. He kissed her sweetly, lovingly, and Kelsey nearly melted. This wasn't mindless passion, the heated exchanges they'd shared in the stairway, but instead a kiss of comfort and longing and sweet seduction. She opened her mouth slightly, inviting him to further the intimacy, and he complied, his tongue engaging hers in a slow, seductive dance.

Kelsey didn't want the kiss to end. But when it finally did, Mitch didn't jerk away from her. Instead he closed his eyes and moved slightly so his cheek rested against her temple. She felt his heart pounding under her fingertips, which had somehow found their way to his shirt-clad chest.

"Mitch?" she whispered against the side of his neck. "Is that how friends usually kiss?"

"I think that's possible," he replied softly.

"Then I'm awfully glad you're my friend."

"WE NEED TO TALK."

Kelsey didn't look up from the pile of correspondence she'd been sorting through. Mitch was obviously trying to keep busy, to cover up the awkward silence that had ensued after their kiss.

"I'm so sick of talking," she replied.

Mitch had been brooding for the past half hour, ever since he'd finally moved away from her and gone back to work. She knew he was trying to figure out what to say, how to rationalize that kiss, and she did not want to hear it.

"We kissed. Friends kiss all the time. You said so yourself. Besides, I think it was natural for us to seek a little emotional release after talking about something so draining. Let's not make more of it than it was, all right?"

Mitch didn't let it go. "Look, Kelsey, there's something happening here, and we need to sort it out."

Kelsey nodded, sighing, giving in. They'd have to have this conversation sooner or later. "I understand,

Mitch. I think, for the first time, I truly understand what you're feeling."

"You do? Tell me, would you?" he said with a self-deprecating smile as he popped a handful of peanuts into his mouth.

"You want me so bad it's killing you."

Mitch choked, and Kelsey jumped up and pounded him on the back.

"Excuse me?" he said when he'd finally stopped coughing.

"You heard me. There's no harm in admitting an attraction, Mitch. You want me. I know because I feel the same way about you."

"That's comforting," he said, an amused grin crossing his face.

"And I finally understand why you have fought the attraction and made every effort to avoid me. I always figured you just saw me as a kid, a brat who used to bug you. But it's a lot deeper than that, right? It's all mixed up in your head, your loyalty to Nathan, your feelings for my parents, your view of yourself as an outsider."

He stared at her, saying nothing, but Kelsey knew she was right.

"It's okay," she insisted. "Now that I know you're not just being a tease, and you have deep reservations about anything happening between us, I can accept your rejections for what they are and not take them personally."

She sounded so logical again. He really couldn't stand it when she made things that were so very complicated sound so very simple. But Mitch couldn't argue with her. She'd cut through all the extraneous garbage floating around in his head, and leaped straight to the correct conclusion. Then what she'd said sank in.

"Tease? What do you mean by that?"

"Well, aren't men allowed to be called that? I mean, if I were the one who kept grabbing you and kissing you and rubbing all over your body and then running away, that's what I'd be called, right? And isn't that what you've been doing?" she asked matter-of-factly.

"Absolutely not! Besides, it's not the same."

"Why not? Because I'm a woman?"

"Exactly," he replied before he could think better of it.

"I'll have you know, *Mr. Hotshot Anthropologist*, that women can have the same physical sensations as men. You'd think, with all the cultures you've studied, you'd have learned that women have needs, too. When you kiss me, when you touch me and I feel your body pressing into mine, all I can think about is making love with you. And when you walk away, it's frustrating as hell. Of course, now that I understand what the problem is, I can let it go. I can wait, Mitch."

"Wait?"

"Yes," she nodded. "Wait for you to come to your senses. But be warned. The next time you start kissing and touching me, you'd better plan to follow through, because I'm not going to let you walk away from me again."

"You're not going to let me—"

"Nope," she said, not allowing him to finish.

"Let me get this straight. You think you can just wait, and I'll totally forget my sense of responsibility and loyalty and fall into bed with you?"

"No, of course not. It's not about forgetting anything, it's about recognizing that you're placing too heavy a burden on yourself."

"A burden. Resisting you is a terrible burden?"

"Uh-huh," she said happily. "But like I said, I can wait. We'll just be friends, as we decided last night. Good friends."

"And if that's all we ever are?"

Kelsey laughed and rolled her eyes as if he'd just made a colossal joke. "Well, *if* that's all, then we'll have a terrific, lifelong friendship."

All he could do was nod. He felt as if he were on a roller coaster, but with Kelsey, he often felt that way. She'd practically challenged him to resist her! For a brief second he considered not resisting her at all, but the impulse was gone in a flash.

Every word he'd said to her about his life and his future was true, and her interpretation was dead-on. She was throwing down a gauntlet, but he had no intention of picking it up. Kelsey Logan was off-limits.

"Okay, Kelsey. No more mixed signals. Let's just concentrate on this friendship thing."

"All right, Mitch." Kelsey kept her eyes downcast so he wouldn't spot the excitement she knew sparkled there.

Nodding and looking slightly relieved, Mitch went back to work. Kelsey watched him try to ignore her while he read some newspapers, translating the Chinese figures laboriously. She liked the intensity of his gaze and how his brow furrowed in concentration. A man with brains was incredibly sexy. And Mitch had brains to spare. Of course the fact that he had the looks to match the brains made him that much more devastating.

And now, she greatly feared, he'd gone and tugged

on her heartstrings. It was bad enough when she just suffered from a teenage infatuation, then a woman's major physical attraction. Now she wanted more than simply the satisfaction she knew they'd find in bed. She wanted him to care about her, to continue opening up to her about subjects dear to his heart. She liked that he confided in her, liked that he trusted her. Now all she had to do was get him to admit that his reluctance to getting involved with her was misplaced.

"Um, Mitch?"

Mitch glanced up quickly, and she knew he'd been waiting for her to break the silence hanging in the room like a shroud.

"I wonder, if, as my very dear *friend*, you could do me a tremendous favor."

"What's that?" he asked.

"Go on a date with me. Whoa, whoa," she continued quickly, holding up her hands in response to his look of suspicion. "I don't mean a date, date. I need an escort."

"For what?"

"The station is a big sponsor of the Wilson College Halloween Ball, and I've been asked to appear."

"Oh, so I'll be escorting Lady Love?"

"Is that such a problem?"

"Look, Kelsey, we've gotten past one major hurdle and agreed to try to get along. Let's not start another argument this soon. You know very well how I feel about your job."

"Yes, I do," she admitted, "and that's why I hoped you'd help me out. This is Lady Love's first appearance in public and, frankly, I'm a little nervous. I could use a friendly face."

That was completely true. She wasn't ready to admit it to him yet, but Mitch had been right about the fact that she might be drawing attention from some undesirable sources.

Kelsey received a great deal of fan mail at the station. Much of it was complimentary. Some letters were flirtatious, the writers often telling her they'd like to help her with some "research." Harmless, really. One writer, who'd written a dozen times, signed his letters "Knight of Your Life" and sent some truly awful poetry proclaiming she was his sun, moon and stars. That particular poem had gone on to say her eyes shone as brightly as the headlights of cars. Brian had laughed aloud for five solid minutes, but Kelsey was touched by the author's earnest sentiment, if not his skills as a poet. He'd been very faithful: she'd been getting letters from him since her very first week on the air.

But lately some of her mail had been a little disturbing. She had heard from jail inmates, and from men who told her very explicitly how they wanted to help Lady Love enhance her sexual knowledge.

Kelsey had already met with Jack, the station manager, about the problem. He'd hired another security guard to assist Edgar, the regular security guy, particularly during her shift. Jack had also offered to have one of them escort her to the Halloween ball, but she'd turned him down. She wasn't ready to allow some sick creeps to dictate how she'd live her life. Neither, however, was she ready to show up at the party alone.

"Won't others from the station be going, as well?" Mitch asked.

"Yes," she said, "but they all will be bringing significant others, and since I don't have one, I feel I'll be a target for any single guy who wants to cash in on some of Lady Love's knowledge."

"So you do realize that some of the attention you're getting is not positive?"

"Of course I do," she answered, shifting her gaze uncomfortably.

Kelsey didn't want to be dishonest, but she also didn't want Mitch any more worried than he already was. She couldn't tell him everything that was going on.

"Look Mitch," she finally said, "we disagree about what I do. But I have no argument with you about the fact that I've put myself in a position where I might draw unwanted admirers."

"Well, I guess we're getting somewhere," Mitch murmured.

He really didn't want to go. Mitch didn't care for college functions anymore, neither the boring faculty ones, nor the raucous student ones. And the Halloween ball, usually held at a downtown hotel, was traditionally a combination of both.

But Kelsey needed him. He couldn't refuse. And it absolutely would not be a date. He'd be simply a stand-in for Nathan, he decided, a male body to run interference between Kelsey and any overzealous fan.

"All right, I'll come. But don't try to put me in costume."

"You have to wear a costume! They're not letting anybody in who's not in costume."

Mitch rolled his eyes and shrugged his shoulders in resignation. "I suppose I could come up with something, though I have no idea how, since the party's next week and I'm absolutely swamped with work."

"Don't you worry about a thing," she assured him.

"You're doing me a big favor by coming, so I will take care of your costume. I'm sure we've got something at the station that will fit you. As a matter of fact, I seem to remember seeing a biker outfit, lots of black leather and chains..."

"Oh, no, no leather." Mitch held his hands up in protest. "I am sure I'll be seeing colleagues and perhaps even former students at this party. Nothing too outrageous, please? Just traditional Halloween fare? A sheet with two holes might work."

"Or it could be a sheet with twenty holes," she replied, "and you could go around saying, 'I got a rock.'"

Her reference came to mind instantly, and he laughed. "That's me, Charlie Brown...and, hey, I see a definite resemblance between you and Lucy."

"Ha, ha, very funny. I wasn't that bad, was I?"

"Kels, you want the truth, or you want me to lie?" he asked with mock sincerity.

"Maybe we'd better just forget I asked."

"Good idea," he said.

"Anyway, I thought maybe you saw me as the little red-haired girl."

"You'd like that, wouldn't you? Me the big, goofy male pining away for the beautiful unattainable girl."

"I'm not unattainable, Mitch," she said softly.

She lowered her lashes, casting him a sultry glance, and Mitch took a step back. "Knock it off." He pointed a finger at her. "Friends, remember?"

She gave a deep, exaggerated sigh and stretched like a cat. "Oh, well, can't blame a girl for trying."

Mitch watched the sinuous movement of her body, and was hit in the stomach with another rush of excitement. "What am I going to do with you?"

"Mitch, stop throwing out openings like that one if you don't want me to come back at you with some very specific suggestions."

Her words brought lots of specific suggestions to his head, and he closed his eyes to picture them. Kelsey in a white negligee, Kelsey in the bath, Kelsey in his arms...Kelsey everywhere!

When he finally opened his eyes, he saw her staring at him intently. Their eyes locked for a moment, then she slowly smiled at him, challenging him to tell her what was on his mind.

"You really are very wicked, Kelsey Logan."

"Maybe that's why you like me so much," she retorted.

Kelsey broke the stare and walked toward the door. "I really need to get out of here. If I've got two costumes to plan, I'd better get started."

"I appreciate your help," he said, following her to the door.

"Anytime, *friend*," she said, "anytime."

7

"So, HAVE YOU GOT ANY IDEA what to dress up as?"

Kelsey glanced at Celia and then continued chopping vegetables. She'd invited the other woman over for dinner. Fred had been working so many hours that Celia hadn't been around the brownstone too much lately. Kelsey missed her.

Plus, she knew Celia was very skilled at sewing.

Celia tossed Kelsey a freshly washed cucumber and started rinsing some lettuce. The two had decided on big salads and worked assembly-line fashion in Kelsey's small kitchen.

"Not a clue," Kelsey said, sighing. "You're the one who can sew. What do you think?"

"I don't know," Celia answered as she turned off the tap water. "Depends on what you're after. Scary? Funny? Outrageous?"

"I suppose," Kelsey responded, "that Lady Love ought to show up in something a little outrageous, probably a little sexy."

"A little sexy?"

"Okay, okay, a lot sexy!"

Celia nodded. "We can do that. What about Mitch?"

"I have no idea," Kelsey said. "He doesn't want anything too flamboyant, so I guess my Adam and Eve idea with suitably placed fig leaves is out."

Kelsey loaded up two plates with salad and fresh vinaigrette, grated some Italian cheese and handed one plate to Celia. Pouring two glasses of Chablis, she offered one to her guest and sat down with her at the kitchen table.

Celia took a few bites of her salad. "I can picture Adam and Eve. Hmm, do they make fig leaves big enough?"

Kelsey feigned indignation. "Celia, I'm not that big!"

"I didn't mean for you," Celia replied, dangling her fork off the end of her fingers and giving Kelsey a sly look.

Kelsey caught her drift and laughed. "Yeah, well, I wouldn't know about that."

"But you'd like to," Celia insisted.

"No comment," Kelsey said, turning her attention to her dinner to avoid dwelling on the picture Celia's words brought to mind.

They both looked up when they heard a loud banging coming from the front door of the brownstone. "Do you know if Fred was expecting someone?" Kelsey asked.

"No, but maybe he or Mitch forgot their keys."

"Could be," Kelsey said, dropping her napkin. As she quickly descended the wooden stairs to the foyer, the knock continued in an almost imperious repetition. Kelsey paused to look through the peephole.

"Oh, great." She sighed aloud when she recognized the blonde who had been in Mitch's apartment that night Kelsey had burst in. She hadn't seen the woman around since, and had begun to hope Mitch wasn't dating her after all. Kelsey contemplated going back upstairs and not answering, but her good manners won out and she opened the door.

"Well, thank you so much," the woman said in a brisk voice. "I've been knocking for five minutes, and it's very chilly out here."

She tried to push past Kelsey to enter the brownstone, but Kelsey blocked her. "Can I help you?"

"I'm here to see Mitch," the blonde said.

"He's not here."

"Well, when will he be back?" The woman was obviously annoyed at being kept standing on the doorstep.

"I have no idea. We don't exactly keep track of each other's comings and goings."

The woman eyed her again, and Kelsey almost wished she'd bothered with a little more makeup and hadn't pulled her hair into a ponytail while making dinner. This statuesque blonde reeked money, looking every bit as lovely as she had the last time she'd been over. Her knee-length coat was obviously cashmere, and she carried a Gucci bag. Her hair was perfectly in place, and her makeup impeccable.

"Give him this, please," she said, shoving something toward Kelsey with one leather-glove-clad hand. "It's his invitation to the Halloween ball. Tell him I am counting on him to come, Kelly."

"It's Kelsey."

"Of course." The woman offered her an insincere smile. "Kelsey, Mitch's friend's sister. He has, of course, told me all about how your family was so kind to him. And how he felt so obligated to rent you a room here to repay them."

Obligated? Mitch felt obligated? Kelsey began to see red. Just then Mitch's car swung up the driveway, and the blonde glanced over her shoulder and smiled in relief. They watched him park his car and start toward the house. Some imp of mischief made Kelsey say, "He's here now, and you can offer the ticket, but I don't think he needs it."

"Oh?" the woman asked, raising her eyebrow imperiously. "Why do you say that?"

"Mitch has a date for the ball. He's going with me. And I've already got tickets."

"You're not serious!"

"About what?" Mitch asked as he walked up the two steps to the front door of the brownstone.

Amanda turned to him and shrilly announced, "Your little 'pseudo-sister' here claims you're attending the Halloween ball with her."

"Of course, she's serious." He scowled at Amanda in annoyance. Sometimes the woman could be incredibly high-handed, as well as thick-skinned. In spite of what had happened the last time she'd come to his apartment, she still continued to call him every few days. He'd avoided complete rudeness, up to now.

"But you *always* go with me, Mitch! And Daddy... he was so looking forward to joining us."

Always could be translated as twice. Mitch had gone with Amanda once, last year, and as a guest of her father's the year before.

"I'm looking forward to seeing him, too. But as I've said, I am going with Kelsey. Her station is sponsoring the event, and she needed an escort."

Amanda's face tightened as she tried to smile. Kelsey figured it took a great deal of effort to turn and say, "I'm sorry for doubting you, Kelsey. Of course Mitch would step in and play the gallant escort."

"Oh, Mitch is nothing if not gallant," Kelsey said.

"But, Mitch," Amanda said, "after Kelsey's finished her duties for her employer, you must join us. Daddy and I will still save you a place at our table."

Amanda cast another glance at Kelsey. "And if Kelsey wishes to remain at the party after she's finished working, she's welcome to sit with us, too."

"How kind," Kelsey murmured, feeling like the unwelcome servant invited to a dinner party to make up for a no-show guest.

The woman did not seem to notice her sarcasm and continued. "However, I do insist that you let me plan your costume, Mitch. I thought we could go as Fred and Ginger again, since everyone loved our costumes last year."

"I'm afraid not. Kelsey is already working on our costumes."

"Oh, Mitch, don't be silly," Amanda replied, undeterred. "It won't matter what costume you wear to play escort for a brief time for your little friend. Your duties shouldn't take too long, then you can join me in your top hat and tails. You won't be chained to Kelsey all night!"

Kelsey figured she ought to have her brain examined for taking the insults that had been flying her way for the past several minutes. "You know, I think I'll leave you two to sort this out, all right? Celia's waiting upstairs. Good night, it was lovely seeing you again."

Not waiting for a reply, she stalked up the stairs, slamming her apartment door behind her.

"My goodness, I hope I didn't offend her, Mitch."

"How could you not have offended her?" Anger made his voice tight and hard. "You walked in here, into Kelsey's home, and started treating her like an unwanted guest, or as if you have some claim to my time, when you know that's absolutely untrue."

"Well," Amanda sputtered, unable to come up with anything else to say. Mitch knew it was pretty stupid to antagonize her. After all, she and her father could easily prevent his books from being required in any class at several colleges.

When he didn't respond or apologize, Amanda said quietly, "I suppose you're right. I'm sorry, Mitch. I was a little abrupt with her. I guess I still am proprietorial about you. Silly of me."

"Maybe you'd better tell Kelsey that next time you see her."

Amanda nodded, said goodbye and walked back to her car.

Mitch let himself into his apartment, wondering if he should go upstairs and straighten things out with Kelsey. She'd mentioned Celia was waiting, so he figured this wouldn't be the best time.

The urge to seek her out had been with him ever since she'd left his place that afternoon. He was getting very used to that urge: it seemed to be constant. For about the twentieth time, Mitch wondered what kind of fool he was to take her to the party. And for about the twenty-fifth time, he told himself there was no way in hell he was going to back out.

"WE WON'T BE CHAINED together all night," Kelsey muttered as she entered her apartment and caught Celia's eye. "Mitch and I won't be chained together at the ball, so of course he can feel free to dump poor little old obligation me and go waltz off with Miss Moneybags and her father!"

Celia looked at her as though she were crazy, and

Kelsey briefly related the conversation with Mitch and his girlfriend.

"So she expects Mitch to ditch you and spend the rest of the evening with her?"

"Apparently so."

"But, Kelsey, Mitch isn't even dating her anymore. Fred told me they broke up before Mitch left town."

Kelsey breathed a deep sigh of relief. She'd suspected as much, but it was good to hear her suspicion confirmed.

"Chained together, indeed," she muttered.

Then an idea began to take shape in her mind. It was outrageous. He'd kill her. But she couldn't stop thinking about it.

"Celia, I think I may have come up with a costume idea after all."

"Really? Fill me in."

Laughing, Kelsey did exactly that. And when she finished explaining what she had in mind, Celia gasped, then laughed, too.

THE NEXT MORNING, armed with a pad of paper and a measuring tape, Kelsey went downstairs and found Mitch in the kitchen.

"How big are you?"

Mitch dropped the bowl he'd been about to put away, and gaped at her. "Excuse me?"

"I'm glad that was plastic," she said, glancing toward the bowl on the floor. "And I said, how big are you? You know, sizes. I've got some costume ideas, but I really need your measurements."

"Oh," Mitch said. "Clothing sizes."

"Uh-huh…what else would I have meant?"

"I have no clue, Kelsey."

Kelsey grinned at his too-innocent tone, then started writing down his sizes as he rattled them off. She probably could have gone with her original guesses, because she had just about hit them dead-on, except for the chest size. She had overestimated that by a bit, probably because she'd gotten so worked up remembering him in her apartment Saturday night wearing that towel. His chest had seemed to go on forever.

"So what's your idea, anyway?" he asked.

She was not about to tell him specifically what she had in mind, but didn't lie, either. "Just a good old Halloween pirate."

"What are we talking here, an Errol Flynn type of pirate? Or more of a Captain Hook with long black curls and high buckle shoes?"

"Definitely Flynn." She didn't want him waving a hook around, especially considering what she'd planned for the rest of the costume.

"By the way, don't shave Saturday, okay? The dark and swarthy look suits you."

Mitch's firm jaw was slightly stubbled; she could tell he hadn't shaved yet. The dark shadow didn't look unkempt, but instead made him look a little rough and exciting. It brought out the hollows under his high cheekbones and accentuated the tiny cleft in his chin. He seemed like the dark, dangerous Mitch she used to know.

"What are you going to wear?" Mitch asked as he moved to dry another dish.

"That's for me to know and you to find out," she said with a secretive smile. "Stand still, let me confirm the measurements you gave me...men have a habit of overestimating sizes."

"Are you always so utterly outrageous?" Mitch couldn't resist laughing at her suggestive words.

She didn't reply as she pulled the measuring tape out and stretched it across his back and shoulders.

"Hurry up, would you?" Having Kelsey leaning against him was very disconcerting. Her hands ran over him lightly, almost teasing him, and her soft breasts pressed into his back. He was very conscious of the contact. When she finally finished, he breathed a deep sigh of relief and stepped away.

"Now, you're not going to back out on me, are you?" she asked.

"I wouldn't dream of it, Kelsey. This whole evening is starting to sound interesting."

KELSEY SPENT THE REST of the day ordering things and sewing. Her plan was pulling together quite nicely. Jack, her boss, called late in the afternoon, anxious to find out if she'd decided how "Lady Love" would be dressed for her first public appearance. Though at first he didn't seem to understand what she described, she said, "Just picture a romance novel cover, all right?" and he finally got it.

That evening at the station, she and Brian quickly threw together some highlights from their discussion Saturday night. When they'd nailed down a topic and listed some songs, Brian sat back and stared at her, a knowing look in his eyes.

"There's talk in the coffee room that you've gotten some more mail from your lovesick knight, Sir He Who Cannot Write Poetry," he said. "Why didn't you share?"

She gave him a sour stare. "Because I knew you'd just make fun of the poor guy. This one was very sweet, too, and we all know how catty you are around genuine sweetness!"

"That's because it doesn't exist," he sniped. "So, does this one compare your voice to the dulcet tones of his grandpappy's harmonica?"

Kelsey pulled out the pale blue stationery. "Actually, it's another poem, in which he claims 'the only sounds bringing tears of joy he'd wipe, are my gravelly voice and a Scottish bagpipe.'"

After Brian let out a few shouts of laughter, he wiped the corners of his eyes. "Oh, man, I wonder if this guy's a comedian...he must be doing it on purpose. No way could someone write such genuinely awful poetry!"

"It's kind of sweet," Kelsey insisted, trying to keep a straight face. "He's writing me two or three times a week now, and he obviously puts a lot of effort into these letters."

"Doesn't that creep you out a little bit? I mean, that someone is crawling out of the woodwork, writing you all these love letters, when he's never even laid eyes on you?"

Kelsey shrugged, folded the letter and slipped it back into its matching blue envelope. "I guess it goes with the territory. There are a lot of lonely people out there who don't have anything better to do than write unrequited love letters."

Brian leaned toward her and took her hand, suddenly serious. "Kelsey, listen, don't take this too lightly, okay? It might seem like nothing to worry about now, but we have all heard stories of overzealous fans going too far."

Kelsey saw genuine concern in Brian's face and squeezed his fingers reassuringly. "There's nothing to worry about. The guy's harmless. Besides, the security guards are being great, I feel totally safe while I'm here."

He smirked. "And, of course, while you're at home, you have a modern-day replica of a Greek god running around in nothing but a towel to protect you. Hey, maybe he's your knight."

"Don't I wish," Kelsey said with a chuckle. "Unfortunately, Mitch was out of the country and had never heard of Lady Love when I started getting the letters."

"Too bad," Brian said as they left the break room. "By the way, you never did fill me in on what happened after I left Saturday night."

"I figured you'd get around to that sooner or later, but it'll have to be later. We've got two minutes and I have to run to the ladies' room," Kelsey said as she hurried away.

"Chicken," Brian called out, his laughter following her down the hall.

MITCH DIDN'T GET MUCH SLEEP for the rest of the week. He spent his days writing, researching or speaking with contributing editors. Though really only in the outline stage, he was pleased with the book's progress.

His long nights were spent listening to the radio. He tried to resist. Every night he promised himself he'd listen to her opening, hear what she was planning to talk about, then shut off the radio. But he never did. He always ended up sticking with Lady Love until her sign-off. The leather living room sofa wasn't very comfortable, so Mitch bought a boom box and put it in his bedroom. Every night he went to bed with Kelsey. Well, with her voice anyway.

As he listened, Mitch's appreciation for Kelsey's talent grew. Her show was always entertaining, sometimes hilarious, usually very sexy. But Paul had been right. It was never raunchy or in poor taste.

Her subjects changed nightly. On Tuesday, her topic was first love. Wednesday, she lightened things up a bit as dozens of callers detailed their most embarrassing romantic moments. On Thursday, she steamed up his room when she talked about eroticism. And last night, Friday, she opened the phones for a sort of free-for-all. She impersonated that little old lady sex doctor, then a French madam. Callers asked romantic trivia questions. Her audience threw challenge after challenge at her, and she answered with wit and style. Mitch was very impressed.

"HAS MITCH SEEN ANY of this yet?" Celia asked.

Kelsey shook her head and continued sewing. The two of them were finishing off the last bits of the costume. Material, clothing and accessories were strewn over most of Kelsey's apartment. Her home looked like a theater dressing room.

"No. I haven't seen much of him this week."

"That's good. I somehow suspect he might rethink this whole Halloween costume if he saw it too far in advance."

"He already knows what he's wearing...pretty much," Kelsey said with a chuckle.

"How's the hair coming?" Celia asked. "Was it uncomfortable to sleep in last night?"

"A little." Kelsey shook her head lightly. The waxed paper that she'd tightly wound around locks of hair all over her head crinkled with every movement. "But it will be worth it. Wait and see."

After they finished everything, including lowering the neckline of Kelsey's blouse once more, Celia said, "Why don't you let me run Mitch's costume down to him so he doesn't see you before tonight. It might be bad luck. Oh, that's just for weddings, right?"

Kelsey grinned and walked Celia to the door, thanking her profusely for all her help. After the other woman left, Kelsey glanced at the clock and saw it was only two. She took a bath, being careful to avoid getting her wrapped hair wet. She soaked for a long time, then got out and rubbed her body with a fragrant, flowery lotion. Pampering herself yet more, she spent another half hour doing her nails, painting them a ruby red. Finally she took a few minutes and began pulling the wax paper out of her hair.

When she was finished, Kelsey shook her head, laughing in delight at the effect. Crinkly, flowing curls cascaded down her back almost to her bra line, bouncing with every move. After applying her makeup with a heavy hand, she surveyed herself in the mirror. The riot of curls framed her dramatically made-up face. She struck a pose, pursing her lips and lifting an eyebrow. She looked exotic, enticing even. Good. That was just what she was shooting for.

"SHE WANTS TO TORTURE ME," Mitch said aloud as he stared down at the indecently tight pants he'd just put on. They were a shiny black material and fit like a second skin. Mitch wondered if she'd written his measurements down wrong. Probably not. Knowing Kelsey, she'd fully intended for them to be as outrageous as possible. She'd had a mischievous sparkle in her eye lately, and he imagined dressing him in a sexy pirate costume was her way of getting back at Amanda for her high-handed treatment. He couldn't look less like Fred Astaire unless he dyed his hair red and put on a clown suit.

Mitch reached for the rest of the costume Celia had delivered earlier in the day, marveling at how complete it was in every detail. Yanking on the accompanying black leather boots, he wasn't surprised to see they came all the way to his knees, covering the bottom of the obscenely tight pants. The shirt was a little better, he thought as he pulled the flowing material over his head. It was white cotton with long, billowing sleeves that gathered at the wrist and spilled lace over his hands. The front had no buttons, instead lacing up with string from his abdomen to his throat, and he left it loose. Celia had told him the bright red silk scarf was to wear around his hips. Mitch quickly wrapped and tied it. Finally he worked up the nerve to look at himself in the mirror, and his jaw dropped. Then he slowly grinned. He looked like some male stripper dressed up for a woman's pirate fantasy.

"Oh, what the hell," he said, laughing out loud. It was one night. It was Halloween. It was for Kelsey. Tonight, Mitch would be a pirate.

AT A FEW MINUTES BEFORE SEVEN, Kelsey heard a knock on her apartment door. Glancing in the mirror one more time, she quickly checked her makeup and called out, "Just a minute, Mitch."

The long rain cape she'd borrowed from Celia lay on a chair by the door, and Kelsey quickly pulled it on, completely covering herself from head to mid-calf. She tucked a few errant curls against her neck, then buttoned the cape.

"Right on time," she said as she yanked the door

open, determined to get out into the murky hall before he had a chance to see much of her. But her intentions fled as she saw him leaning indolently against the doorframe.

He looked magnificent.

Mitch's thick, dark brown hair was tied back into a short ponytail with a strip of leather. She hadn't made that suggestion, but it worked perfectly, giving him even more of a rakish piratical appearance. He was unshaved, his face dark and lean, giving him a dangerous look. The white shirt gaped open, exposing the crisp dark hair on his hard chest, and her eyes followed the vee down almost to his waist. The tight red sash emphasized his lean build, and the black pants...well, if she started thinking too much about what Mitch looked like in those black pants, they'd never get to the ball.

"What do you think?"

"You look gorgeous...tall, dark and dangerous," she admitted weakly.

He flashed her a boyish grin, and said, "I have to admit I do feel very Errol Flynn-ish. You and Celia did a great job. Where on earth did you find this stuff?"

"Just lucky, I guess. Some of it we put together ourselves, and some I got in the mall. I found the boots in a thrift shop."

"Wait a minute," he said, at last noticing the cape that covered her from the top of her head to her knees. "I want to see your costume."

"No time," she retorted. "We've got to go. And it's raining a little. I don't want to mess up my hair."

Mitch frowned at her, but Kelsey ignored him and grabbed the bag she'd left sitting by the front door.

"What's this?"

"Just some props. Finishing touches to my master-piece."

Kelsey rushed downstairs, glad to hear the rain still hitting the windows. It had given her the perfect ex-cuse to wear the concealing cape. Mitch put his own coat on and opened the door, then glanced down and noticed her shoes.

"What do you have on your feet?"

Kelsey wore flat brown leather sandals. Instead of a buckle, they fastened with two long strips of leather, which she'd wound around her ankles and up her calves.

"Sandals, why?" she asked, offering no explana-tion.

Mitch sighed, glanced at her feet, then at the soggy yard. Not bothering to ask, he bent and picked her up in his arms. She gasped. He shouldered the front door open, and dashed with her across the front yard to his car. She didn't utter so much as a word as he quickly opened the car door and sat her in the passenger seat.

As they drove toward the harbor, Kelsey began hav-ing second thoughts. What if Mitch outright refused to go along with it? It wouldn't really matter, she sup-posed. They would both still be in costume, though hers might look a little strange. His pirate outfit would be fine. In fact, she acknowledged, this whole thing might blow up right in her face. Because if he balked at using her "props," he would very likely be a target for every single woman in the place, Amanda included. She wished for a moment that she hadn't done such a good job on his costume.

"Looks like a big crowd," he said when they pulled up to the hotel entrance and he stopped in front of the valet parking stand. "Do you see anyone from work?"

Kelsey glanced through the raindrops on the car windshield and saw several costumed party goers. A man dressed in a green Godzilla costume stood out, but everyone else was indistinguishable.

The hotel was an elegant structure that had stood in the downtown area for probably forty years or more. Kelsey had read that the building had recently been renovated, and the interior gleamed. Casting an appreciative eye around the plush lobby, she noted a few costumed guests mingling in one corner, while a family with two impatient children checked in at the front desk. Leather sofas were arranged in intimate groupings, and a couple sat whispering to each other in one of them. An impeccably uniformed porter bustled toward the elevator, while sparkling lights reflecting off the crystal chandelier danced across his mauve uniform.

Mitch moved toward the coat check, but Kelsey caught hold of his sleeve. "Could you come here for a minute? I need to finish setting us up."

"Setting us up?"

Kelsey led him across the thick gold carpeting to a corridor opposite the lobby. They slipped into a small alcove near the game room. The wall was mirrored, and the area well lit. Perfect.

"Are you going to tell me what's going on?" he asked as she dropped the satchel to the floor. "You've been acting very mysteriously."

"I know. But all will now be revealed." She bit her lip nervously. Kelsey caught Mitch's eye as she began unbuttoning her cape. She gently pulled the hood back, revealing her curls, then let the cape slide from her shoulders to pool around her feet.

Mitch sucked in his breath and widened his eyes.

She wore a gauzy white blouse that clung to her body as if it were painted on. Only the sleeves, long and billowy, were loose. They covered her from upper arm to wrist. But her shoulders, upper chest, and throat were totally exposed. The top of the tight blouse skimmed her breasts, revealing a great deal of creamy cleavage, and Mitch thought if Kelsey moved too quickly she would reveal far more than she wanted to.

Adding to the natural "spillage" danger was the fact that Kelsey wore a tight white bustier over the blouse. It laced in the front, cinching her waist to near nothingness, hugging her midriff and pushing her breasts up to a dangerous level.

A flowing white skirt skimmed over her shapely hips and fell in layered ruffles to mid-calf. Kelsey moved slightly, and Mitch saw that on one side the skirt curved into a slit that came up to her upper thigh.

Her hair was a mass of shining curls, lustrous and inviting and seductive as hell, falling in ringlets over her shoulders. Her huge green eyes stared at him from her exquisite face, and Mitch just drank in her beauty.

"What in heaven's name are you supposed to be?" he finally asked when he regained the ability to speak.

Kelsey dropped her eyes and said, "Um...your wench."

"My what?"

"You know," she explained, "a pirate's wench."

"A...pirate's wench?"

Kelsey bent over, and Mitch was unable to suppress a groan at the view he was given. He watched as she grabbed for the bag she'd had him carry into the lobby.

"Now, Mitch, you trust me, right?"

Mitch was able to nod, but that was all. His voice

hadn't started working yet, since she'd sucked all the air out of his body when she bent over in front of him.

"Okay, then," she said, "close your eyes."

Mitch complied instantly, glad for the chance to pull his eyes back into his head.

"Just bear with me, okay? Withhold judgment for a minute?"

"I'll agree to withhold judgment if you'll agree not to fall out of that damned blouse," he said without opening his eyes.

A light peal of laughter was her only response. The bag she'd been carrying rustled, then Mitch heard a clinking sound and tried to place it. It registered about two seconds before he felt the shackle slide around his wrist and snap shut with a click.

"What the…"

"Uh-uh, no peeking. Just one more second," Kelsey said, sliding the other shackle over her own wrist. "Now you can open your eyes."

Mitch did.

They stood in front of a mirrored wall, and Mitch studied the reflection. Kelsey stared at him in the mirror, biting the corner of her lip and looking the tiniest bit uncertain. As well she might.

"Kelsey, we're chained together."

"Yes, Mitch, I know."

8

MITCH'S RIGHT WRIST WAS ENCASED in a metal bracelet that looked and felt like a real prisoner's shackle. About five feet of chain, probably three-quarter-inch links, hung down his body, then looped and traveled up Kelsey's white-clad form, ending at a smaller shackle on her left wrist.

Though there was enough play in the chain for them to move apart, Kelsey was pressed against him, still watching for his reaction. Mitch took a deep breath, inhaling her flowery fragrance, and felt a familiar rush of excitement. He continued to study the reflection. He and Kelsey, a pirate and a wench.

"Well?" she finally asked, breaking the several moments of silence. "What do you think?"

"Hmm," he said slowly, "what do I think?"

He saw her mouth tighten and her hand move toward her pocket. She was nervous. He figured she was about to reach for the keys.

"I think," he finally said, "that we look pretty damn good."

"Oh, I love you! I knew you'd be a good sport about this," Kelsey said as she laughed and pulled him down for a quick kiss on the mouth.

Some devil inside him made him tighten his arms around her waist and deepen the kiss. Mitch didn't question the impulse as he pressed his mouth against hers. She didn't seem to question it, either, because she immediately tilted her head and parted her lips invitingly.

He was alive with sensation, following his instincts instead of his intellect and it felt *so* good. As did she. She molded against him perfectly, pressing her body against his from neck to hip. This time when they finally drew apart, Mitch didn't regret the kiss for one second.

"Ready, wench?" he asked, glancing at Kelsey's swollen lips, then lowering his gaze to her heaving chest.

"Oh, yeah, I'm ready," she muttered. "I think you are, too."

Mitch followed her frank gaze down the front of his own body. His black pants left absolutely nothing to the imagination, and certainly no room for arousal.

"You better give me a minute before we go inside," he said, his voice a throaty whisper.

"I'd give you a lot longer than that if we weren't standing in a public hallway."

"Hell, Kelsey, the way I'm feeling right now, I probably wouldn't *need* much longer than that!"

She laughed softly. Mitch pulled his gaze off her and stared at the ceiling, trying to calm himself down by thinking of Chinese burial rituals, bowls of cold oatmeal and his first-grade teacher, a gray-haired old battle-ax named Mrs. Dora. Finally he looked at her and nodded. "Let's do it."

A slow, wicked smile spread across her face.

"I mean," he said, narrowing his eyes, "let's go to the ball, Lady Love."

"Is that what makes tonight different?" she asked.

"Am I just Lady Love tonight, and can you forget about the fact that I'm Kelsey Logan?"

Her lips were parted and he watched as the tip of her tongue slid out to moisten them. She moved closer, laying her hand flat against his chest, and stared up at him with liquid desire in her eyes. The conservative college professor in him tried to answer logically, but his brain and vocal cords didn't connect.

"Keep looking at me like that, *Lady Love*, and you're not going to make it to the ball."

Kelsey felt a rush of triumph fill her. "Who says I want to?"

He shook his head, then chuckled. "Come on, little wench. You need to keep your job to pay your rent."

Kelsey sighed, picked up the empty bag she'd used to carry the chain, and let him lead her out of the alcove.

"I guess this means I won't be doing much dancing with 'Ginger' tonight, hmm?" Mitch asked as he jiggled the chain.

Kelsey flushed lightly as she realized Mitch knew exactly why she'd come up with the costume idea. "Well, we don't have to leave them on all evening. I'm supposed to spend an hour greeting people and giving out promotional stuff. After that, we're on our own."

"Let's see what happens, all right? We'll definitely stick together while Lady Love is working."

Kelsey gave him one more chance to back out. "You're sure about this? I mean, it might be a little embarrassing."

"Baby, let me tell you, being chained to a beautiful woman who calls herself my wench is only going to enhance my reputation," Mitch assured her. "Now, let's go. I'm sure all of Baltimore is anxious to meet the infamous Lady Love."

Kelsey nodded and they walked back toward the lobby. A brunette dressed as Cleopatra sat cozily with a man who looked like a punk rocker on one of the sofas in the lobby. The queen of Egypt stared at Mitch as they walked by. The harried-looking mommy of two, still standing at the front desk, couldn't keep her eyes off him, either. Kelsey curled her fingers in his possessively.

The chain clinked a little as they walked, but Kelsey ignored it, proceeding as if she and Mitch were just like any other couple holding hands in a hotel lobby…half-dressed and chained together.

"Where do we go first? Do we find a table or do you report for duty?"

Kelsey glanced at the clock hanging above the double doors leading into the ballroom. "We're right on time. I'm supposed to work for the first hour."

"Does the station have a booth or something?"

"Yeah. And my boss left me a note that they're setting up a special area for me."

Mitch was moving to open the door for her when a group of twenty or so people came from behind them, laughing and complimenting one another's costumes. The group moved toward the doors, sweeping Mitch and Kelsey right along with them into the ballroom.

Inside, Kelsey glanced quickly around the huge parquet-floored room. There was a large crowd standing in a buffet line, and most of the tables were already full. Several couples were on the dance floor. Along the far right wall she saw a large banner with the call letters for the station, and they steered along the outside edge of the ballroom as they made their way toward it.

"Kelsey!"

Glancing around, Kelsey saw Brian approaching them. He was dressed as a large chicken and looked about as uncomfortable as anyone she had ever seen.

"Hi, Brian. You look…interesting," Kelsey said, trying unsuccessfully to suppress a grin.

"Don't get me started," Brian responded with a sour look. "I reserved the Lone Ranger and Tonto costumes for Chuck and me, but the rental place messed up and I had to choose from what was hanging on the racks. I'm the chicken, and Chuck is dressed up as Godzilla."

"I thought that lizard looked familiar," Kelsey said.

"You need to hurry up. The station photographer's taking a few shots over at the booth and wants you in them. Sweetie, you two look great…I can't wait to see you in the cover."

"The cover?" Kelsey asked, not knowing what he was talking about. Brian hurried away without responding.

Mitch didn't protest as Kelsey squeezed through the crowd, dragging him behind her. They generated stares throughout the length of the ballroom, and Mitch nodded to a few familiar faces, chuckling at their astonishment at his appearance. He grinned at the college dean, who was dressed as a vampire. The man's jaw dropped so hard when he saw a chained Mitch being led by Kelsey that his false fangs popped out and landed with a bubbling fizz in his drink. Mitch imagined there would be a new topic of conversation at the next faculty party.

As they approached the large WAJO banner, which

Mitch could see over the heads of people pressed near the radio station's booth, they skirted between a few tables and came up from behind to avoid the crowd. Kelsey introduced Mitch to two of the other deejays already there, then waved at a photographer standing nearby.

"Perfect timing, Kels. I want to finish off this roll, and I've got to get out of here soon," Dan said. "You don't have a problem with me taking a few shots for the station, do you?" he asked, obviously addressing Mitch.

"I guess not," Mitch replied.

"Good," Dan said. "I just need you to sign the standard forms."

Mitch watched as the man felt around his camera bag and came up with two small crumpled-looking pieces of paper and a pen. Kelsey signed first, without bothering to read the card, and Mitch followed suit. His signature ended up a crooked scrawl because Kelsey accidentally jerked the chain while he wrote. "Watch it, wench," he muttered.

"Sorry, master," she said with a saucy grin. "Are you going to punish me later?"

Their eyes met for one charged moment. "Only if you're lucky."

"Okay, we're all set," Dan said as he shoved the signed forms back into his camera bag. "I have to say, you two look amazing. This is going to be terrific."

"I hope you're right," Kelsey said. "Where do you want us?"

The photographer rolled his eyes. "In the cover, of course, right over here."

Dan grabbed Kelsey and Mitch by their chained hands, pulling them forward to stand beneath a large wooden frame. Kelsey could only see it from the back. She assumed a special "Lady Love" promo was on the front. The frame was about seven feet tall, and contained a large empty spot in the middle. As the photographer pulled them beneath it, Kelsey realized it was built around the shape of two bodies. She and Mitch fit very nicely inside the center cutout.

"Let me pose you, all right?" the photographer asked. Kelsey didn't protest as he grasped her shoulder and turned her to face Mitch, pushing her tight against him. Mitch's eyes opened wider and he looked at her for an explanation, but Kelsey was as confused as he appeared to be.

"Here," Dan said to Mitch, "grab her leg."

Kelsey gasped as Dan pulled her right knee up and placed Mitch's hand high up on the back of her thigh. Their bodies were pressed intimately together, with her leg almost resting on his hip. Before she could say a word, Dan had placed Mitch's arm around her waist and gently pushed Kelsey's shoulders back so Mitch's arm was almost completely supporting her. Then he lifted Kelsey's hand and placed it against Mitch's bare chest. She couldn't resist digging her fingers slightly into the skin next to the soft cotton shirt.

"What are you doing?" Kelsey asked softly, suddenly worried about the extreme seductiveness of the pose.

"Ah, ah," The man held up his hand. "Just let me be creative. Kelsey, toss back that hair, purse those lips of yours. Come on, get into it, you two."

Mitch stared down at Kelsey and caught her eyes with his own. Her lips were parted, her breath coming in short gasps, and Mitch felt another rush of desire for her. Standing in the middle of a crowd of people, all he could think was that if he bent forward a few inches, he could press a hot kiss in the hollow of her throat.

"Yes, yes, that's it," Dan said as he backed away and began focusing his camera.

One of the other deejays approached the microphone and cleared his throat for attention. "Ladies and gentlemen, appearing in public for the first time, WAJO's own princess of the night, Lady Love."

Mitch noticed a perceptible drop in conversation, at least in the tables closest to the booth. The deejay's announcement over the microphone probably didn't reach the far recesses of the huge ballroom, but everyone within at least thirty feet stopped their conversations and turned to watch.

"Look enraptured!" Dan whispered loudly as he began snapping pictures.

A small spotlight came up, illuminating them from head to toe, and Mitch did as Dan ordered, not because of the photographer's request, but because he could do nothing else. He stared down at Kelsey with every ounce of pent-up desire he felt for her. He would have sworn that anyone within five feet could have felt the heat coming from them.

Someone whistled, someone else cheered, and then a loud thunder of applause washed over them. Mitch barely noticed. He studied Kelsey's face, with her full pouty lips and her half-lowered eyelids. She looked like she wanted to be ravished. And he felt more than ready for the job. Suddenly, for some reason, the pose, the costume, her hair, everything…started to look familiar.

"Kelsey," Mitch said as the applause continued,

and flashbulbs popped, "am I standing under what I think I'm standing under?"

Kelsey, who had realized at about the same instant that her innocent words to her boss had been misconstrued and used to design this "stage," nodded weakly.

"Oh, my God. We're a romance novel cover, aren't we?"

She nodded again. Watching as Mitch gritted his teeth, she wondered if he would let go of her waist and let her fall to the floor. She wouldn't really blame him if he did. He probably wanted to strangle her!

After the applause began to die down and the photographer gave Kelsey a thumbs-up, she relaxed a little and tried to pull away from her pirate. He would have none of it.

"Oh, no, you don't," he said. "If I'm going to stand here doing this, I'm sure as hell going to make it worth my time!"

Mitch grabbed Kelsey's hip with one hand, allowing the chain to dangle between them. Thrusting his other hand into her thick curls, he wound his fingers close to her scalp, caressing her slightly before gently tugging her head farther back. Her eyes widened, almost as much as his narrowed, and he jerked her body tighter against his from the waist down. He leaned forward, forcing her to arch her back even farther, and bent toward her bare throat and bosom, stopping with his lips just inches from her flesh.

The crowd began applauding and whistling all over again, and the photographer snapped away. Kelsey felt her back was going to break, but she didn't move. She'd seen a flash of anger in Mitch's eyes and didn't want to risk making it worse. He obviously believed she had planned this entire thing and was paying her back. She probably deserved it. Her comment to her boss about "picturing a romance novel cover" had precipitated this entire mess. But this pose was killing her. Mainly because what she really wanted to do was wrap her fingers in his dark hair and pull him those scant few inches to her breast.

"Well, that's our Lady Love, and her escort. Lady Love will be happy to visit with fans for the next hour, so if you've been wanting to meet her, please come do so."

Mitch heard the deejay make the announcement. Realizing people would be approaching them, he pulled away from Kelsey, drawing her up with him. He didn't trust himself to say anything yet, and tried to paste on a pleasant expression as people surrounded the display.

Kelsey shot him an uncertain glance out of the corner of her eye and whispered, "I didn't know, Mitch. I swear to you...I give you my word...I had no idea they were going to do this."

Mitch recognized the remorse in her voice and knew she was telling the truth. That made the entire embarrassing incident somewhat better. Before he could say a word to reassure her, several ardent fans surrounded the booth and began clamoring for Kelsey's attention.

"THANK YOU, THANK YOU SO MUCH" Kelsey said in reply to the three college students who had complimented her costume, and *Night Whispers*. "I'm glad you like the show. Have any of you called in?"

Mitch cast a quick glance over the three young men who looked more nervous than threatening, and determined that Kelsey had nothing to fear from them. Carefully turning to avoid yanking her with the chain, he slipped out from under the frame to look at it.

Someone had designed and created a complete seven-foot-tall romance novel cover for the ball, leaving only the center cut out so he and she could step into it and complete the picture. The board tacked to the wooden frame was painted a pale lavender, and vines and flowers, very artistically drawn, trailed down both sides. Glittery gold letters spelled out "Pirate's Prisoner of Passion" across the top. There was even a small pirate ship on a stormy sea painted on one side. He could only imagine how the two of them had looked standing in that perfectly measured cutout center during their dramatic pose. A small grin tickled his lips.

Peeking around the bodies of the people pressing to meet her, Kelsey watched Mitch study the frame. He still didn't look too pleased, although she felt sure she'd seen a sparkle of humor. She hadn't worked up the nerve to step out of the frame and examine it from the front yet.

Kelsey continued chatting with fans, most of whom were friendly and nonthreatening. There were one or two, unfortunately, who made some suggestive comments, and Kelsey appreciated that Mitch moved closer, placing his hand on her shoulder, on those occasions. As much as she tried just to enjoy herself, she couldn't help tensing up when any strange man got too close. In the back of her mind, she wondered if it was possible her secret admirer was in the crowd. She kept glancing around, looking for someone dressed as a knight, but didn't spot anyone.

"Excuse me, ladies and gentlemen," Mitch said after nearly two hours. "But I think my captive here needs a break. You will excuse her, won't you?"

Not waiting for a reply, Mitch took Kelsey's elbow and led her away from the crowd. He made his way to a small, unoccupied table on the edge of the ballroom and pulled back a chair.

"Sit. I'm going to go round us up some food and drinks."

Kelsey began to protest, but Mitch ignored her and started to walk away. He made it half-a-dozen steps before being stopped short by the pull of the chain. Glancing ruefully at his wrist, he looked over his shoulder at Kelsey. Her hand was over her mouth in a vain attempt to smother her chuckles.

"We can do this one of two ways," she said as she began pulling the chain hand over hand, shortening the distance between them as Mitch feigned protest. "Stick together and go for food as a team..." she continued.

"Or?"

"Or I pull out the key and release you."

Mitch frowned in thought. He was not ready to be "released" from duty. "Hmm, tough choice. I think maybe we'd better leave the chain for now. I don't trust you enough to let you out of my sight. The next thing I know you'll have me volunteered to go onstage and sing 'The Monster Mash.'"

"I remember hearing you sing in the shower when you were a teenager, and I wouldn't dare!"

"Very funny...coming from Miss Two Left Feet."

"All right, let's call it even," she said. "You can't sing. I can't dance. Together, though, we're very talented."

"Together we're very...*something*."

"Perfect?" Kelsey said with a determined flippancy she didn't feel.

Mitch leaned forward in his chair until their faces were mere inches apart. Her heart started pounding as she recognized the dangerously seductive look on his face.

"Maybe we could be, Lady Love."

She thought for a second he was going to close the gap between them and kiss her again. She leaned imperceptibly closer, silently urging him to do it, not caring that hundreds of people milled around them.

"There you are, Mitch. I've been waiting for you to finish chaperoning Kelsey here. My, my, Kelsey, you certainly are the sly one. Imagine, Mitch's little childhood friend being the infamous Lady Love!"

Kelsey sighed in frustration and glanced up at the sound of Amanda's shrill voice. The blonde stood close to Mitch's chair, breaking the intimate spell they'd been under, as she'd obviously intended.

"Goodness, Mitch," Amanda continued, her saccharine tones irritating Kelsey tremendously. "How on earth did you let Kelsey talk you into helping her with this...well, titillating performance of hers? I don't imagine anyone ever dreamed that this was how you'd end up 'taking care' of your pseudo-sister. My, my, what would the folks back home say?"

Kelsey could see Mitch retreat from her, mentally and physically, as he sat up straighter in his chair and adopted his usual calm expression. The dangerous Mitch she remembered from her childhood was tucked safely back inside and she was going to spend the rest of her evening with the college professor. Kelsey suddenly wanted to punch someone. Someone blond.

It wasn't that she didn't like Mitch the way he was now. She liked him too much, that was part of the problem. He was smart and funny, thoughtful and sensitive, and sexy in the way brainy men are. But when he allowed a little tiny bit of that dark rebel to slip out, he was absolutely irresistible. And only with the rebel would Kelsey have a chance to make him admit how good they could be together.

Amanda's intrusion hit Mitch like a gallon of cold water. The sultry mood was gone. He tried hard not to think of how the night might have ended if he'd gone on pretending he was only with Lady Love. He probably ought to thank Amanda for splashing him with a dose of reality by bringing up the Logan family. But he didn't feel very grateful.

"Amanda, I was just about to ask Kelsey to dance. You will excuse us, won't you?"

Not waiting for her answer, Mitch helped Kelsey up and led her onto the dance floor, brushing aside her protests that she really was a lousy dancer. Pretending she wasn't too bad, he ignored the half-dozen times she stepped on his toes. Bruised toes were a small price to pay for avoiding a major heartache. And the moment he and Kelsey had shared just before Amanda interrupted could easily have led to one major emotional pain.

Throughout the rest of the evening, Mitch treated Kelsey with polite cordiality, and nothing more. They danced a few times, ate a late dinner and had a few drinks. At one point, Kelsey needed to go to the ladies' room, and surrendered the key to the shackles. When she returned, he didn't suggest she rechain them, and neither did she.

Mitch told himself he wasn't disappointed.

9

THE DRIVING RAIN POUNDED against her window, and a crash of thunder reverberated, startling Kelsey awake with a jolt. Sitting up in bed, she stared around in dazed confusion. Then she glanced toward her bedside clock but didn't see the familiar glowing green numbers. It wasn't working. A long flash of lightning illuminated her nightstand. Grabbing her watch, she saw that it was just after two. She'd only been asleep for about an hour.

The storm that had brought drizzling rain all day had arrived with torrential fury. Kelsey shivered a little and pulled the covers up tighter. This old house was very drafty, and in the short time the electricity must have been out her room had become quite chilly. Remembering the spare comforter in the linen closet, she got up to get it, then noticed the streetlamp in front of the house was lit.

"That's funny," she said aloud, staring through the rain-streaked window at the muted yellow glow.

Some other houses had porch lights on, and Kelsey realized the electricity wasn't out after all. It had probably just flickered, causing a breaker to flip in the basement. She thought about grabbing the comforter and going back to bed, but it really was very chilly, and Mitch or Fred might not realize until tomorrow morning that the heat wasn't working.

Kelsey quickly felt around on the floor until she found her slippers. She didn't bother with her robe, since she wore long satin pajamas. Making her way down the short hallway into the kitchen, she pulled open a drawer and located the flashlight she kept there for emergencies. She flicked it on, praying the batteries still worked, and sighed in relief when a weak yellow beam came forth.

Slipping quietly out of her apartment, Kelsey carefully avoided the creakiest steps as she descended the stairs. It was doubtful Mitch would hear her anyway, but she didn't want to risk it. The last thing she wanted was for Mitch to find her lurking in the house in the middle of the night, and be all kind and solicitous, as he'd been at the ball. Mitch had been so darned friendly that she thought she could have cheerfully strangled him! It was as if, in that moment when Amanda had stepped between them, the invisible wall Mitch kept around himself had slipped back into place so firmly it couldn't be blasted away with dynamite.

Kelsey stealthily entered his kitchen, playing the weak beam of light over the butcher-block table so she could maneuver around it.

"Ouch," she muttered as she bumped her shin into a chair.

Limping slightly, she made her way to the basement door, opened it, silently cursing the loud creak, then went down into the basement. The breaker box was in the far corner, past the washing machine, Kelsey remembered. She began walking across the large basement floor when suddenly her flashlight dimmed then went out completely.

"Oh, no," she said as she stopped to allow her eyes

to become accustomed to the pitch-dark. Gradually shadows began to appear, and then a long flash of lightning seeped in through the basement windows along the back of the house. There were no piles of boxes or laundry on the floor before her, so she gingerly began to pick her way across the room.

MITCH'S NOSE WAS COLD. He came slowly out of a deep sleep, realizing that very chilly air circled his face. He heard the thunder first, then the rain, and assumed a breaker had popped, as usual, and knocked out the heat. He'd been fighting to get the electrician he'd had rewire the house to come back to check the breakers, which were very temperamental. Getting out of bed, he pulled a pair of sweatpants over his naked body. He walked to the kitchen, using flashes of lightning to help see the way.

Stopping near the oven, Mitch opened a cabinet and pulled out a box of long wooden kitchen matches. He lit one and began descending the stairs, cupping the match with his hand. The little flame banished the shadows in the stairwell until he reached the bottom. A draft blew it out as soon as his feet touched the cement basement floor. Realizing he should have brought the whole box, he considered going back up to the kitchen for more matches. But he really didn't see the need. He knew this basement very well, and should be able to make his way to the breaker box with little difficulty.

Kelsey felt the tripped breakers, flipped them and was about to head back through the darkened basement when she heard a loud creak at the bottom of the stairs. Someone was down here in the darkness with her. A tiny jolt of fear shot through her, but she quickly told herself it had to be Mitch or Fred.

Standing in the corner of the room, partially concealed behind the washer, Kelsey pressed back deeper into the shadows. Lightning briefly lit the basement with a muted yellow flash, and Kelsey saw Mitch clearly but only for a moment. Then he faded into darkness again, and she strained to follow his movements.

She couldn't tear her eyes off his shadowy figure as he slowly moved toward her. Another streak of lightning flashed through the basement windows and she caught a glimpse of his hard, bare chest and unsmiling face. He obviously hadn't seen her yet, and she made no sound, wanting to appreciate the sight of him for one more moment.

Mitch sensed Kelsey, though he didn't see her. A faint trace of the perfume she'd worn earlier to the ball lingered in the basement, and he knew she was near. He stopped, listening, struggling to hear the sound of her breathing. His own breaths started coming quicker, harder, and his heart began to pound.

Kelsey sensed the moment he discovered her presence. She saw him pause, cocking his head to one side, trying to hear her.

"Kelsey?" he whispered.

She took a deep breath and whispered back, "I'm here, Mitch."

Mitch said nothing but moved toward the dark corner where he'd heard her voice. His eyes grew accustomed to the gloom, and he saw her, silent, motionless, waiting for him. He stopped a few feet from her, but Kelsey took three small, tentative steps toward him until their bodies nearly met. Her warm exhalations brushed the cool skin of his chest, exciting him beyond measure. They didn't touch, yet only the tiniest breath of air separated them. Neither moved. Neither spoke.

Mitch searched through the shadows and the darkness for a glimpse of Kelsey's green eyes. Every ounce of his being longed to move those scant inches and take her in his arms. He waited for the familiar tightening, the voice that would shout, "No, you can't do this," but he heard nothing except the strong beat of his own heart.

Another flash of lightning lit the room, and Mitch saw the naked longing he'd hoped for in Kelsey's face. Her right hand was poised a hairsbreadth from his chest, and only when the room plunged into darkness once again did she move the tips of her fingers in a long caress across his bare skin. Mitch hissed out a clenched breath, nearly undone by her soft touch. When she curled her fingers and lightly brushed her fingernails across his abdomen, he groaned aloud.

Thunder rumbled, rolling across the basement like the steady pounding of a drum. Kelsey's heart beat to its rhythm. In that last bit of light, she saw just what she wanted to in Mitch's face. There would be no turning back, no rejection. Mitch was hers. At last.

Kelsey continued exploring Mitch's hard body, stroking both hands on his chest, then dragging her nails across his ribs. A torrent of emotion seemed to snap in him because suddenly he slid his hands in her hair and turned her face up to his.

"Now, Kelsey," he said, before capturing her mouth with his own.

Mitch's kiss was hard and demanding yet promised delights beyond her fantasies. He twined his fingers in her hair as he devoured her mouth. Kelsey met every sweet, wet thrust of his tongue, telling him wordlessly she was as consumed with passion as he.

Her moans of pleasure turned to whimpers as his hands slid down her body. He teased the skin beneath the satiny pajama top, stroking her soft belly, closing his large hands around her waist, then sliding them up her ribs. Her bare breasts throbbed, aching for his touch, and when he finally cupped them in his hands she thought she'd jump out of her skin.

"Yes, oh, please," she moaned, mindless with pleasure as he ran his palms over her taut, aching nipples.

He stroked her, savoring the soft feel of her flesh. Mitch wanted to taste her, every inch of her. He heard her disappointed moan when he lowered his hands from her breasts, then her excited gasp when she realized he was yanking off her top. Mitch paid no attention. He wrapped one arm around her waist and leaned her back until he could capture the tip of one lovely breast in his mouth.

She thought she might scream. His lips and tongue caressed her, and his teeth lightly scraped her sensitive flesh, sending chills down her spine. Kelsey dug her hands into Mitch's shoulders, leaning even farther back and urging him ever closer, not wanting to lose one moment of sensation. He supported her entire weight. Her feet slipped a bit on the cement, but he held her safe.

Realizing he might be hurting her, Mitch grabbed Kelsey, lifting her by her pajama-clad hips, and pulled her legs around his waist. He held her there, keeping his arms tight around her, taking advantage of her nearness to thoroughly kiss the front of her body. She wriggled against him, pressing against his throbbing erection, and he was overpowered with the need to be inside her.

"Kelsey," he said raggedly as he trailed kisses up her neck to the side of her face. "We need to go upstairs. I don't have anything with me...for protection."

She didn't say a word, just grabbed his hair and pulled his mouth to hers for another long, mind-searing kiss. Mitch walked across the basement floor toward the stairs, carrying her, her long slim legs wrapped tightly around his waist. When she pulled her mouth away to gulp in a lungful of air, Mitch ran the tip of his tongue across her earlobe, down her neck and over her collarbone, before capturing her throbbing breast again. Her hips jerked in an instant response.

He carried her effortlessly up the stairs, her slight weight not hindering him at all. Mitch was so overwhelmed with desire and adrenaline that he probably could have carried her like that for miles. He paused in the kitchen, leaning back against the counter while she rained kisses along his jawline and up to his mouth.

Kelsey boldly kissed Mitch, sucking his bottom lip and exploring him with her tongue. Then they were moving again and she held on, not caring where they went as long as he did not stop this delicious assault on her senses.

Mitch paused as they entered the bedroom, and Kelsey watched as he flicked on the switch to a small lamp on the dresser. The dim light enabled her to see his handsome face clearly, and she felt a rush of feminine pleasure at his look of mindless desire. She glanced over his shoulder into the mirror and almost didn't recognize the wide-eyed woman staring back at her. Her hair, still curly from her costume, was wildly tangled, and her lips were swollen and parted. She watched the muscles of Mitch's back tense and ripple as she slowly ran her fingernails over him.

Mitch yanked a box of condoms out of a dresser drawer and tossed it onto the bed. Slowly he released her, letting her slide down his body without ever breaking their intimate contact. Trying to control his ragged breathing, he gently brushed her hair away from her face and kissed her softly on the temple.

"Maybe we'd better slow down. I don't want to hurt you," he said, trying to force himself to calm down in spite of the torrent of raging emotion still churning inside his body.

"Don't you dare," Kelsey said, turning to press her lips against his once more. She reached her arms around his neck and whispered against his mouth, "You can be gentle next time."

Mitch didn't need any further invitation. Her softly spoken command inflamed him, and he reached for her waist and slid the silky pajama bottoms off her body in one long, slow caress. His knuckles scraped against her, and he realized she wore nothing underneath. The soft feel of her drove the last coherent thought from his mind.

Kelsey slid her hands beneath the elastic waistband of Mitch's sweatpants, pulling them down his legs in one smooth motion. She wrapped her arms around his back, pressing her naked body against his, loving the hard feel of his erection against her belly. Dipping her hands slightly to caress his bare hips, she slid her fingers around to explore him more intimately.

Mitch sucked in his breath at the soft touch of her

hands on his swollen, throbbing flesh. "You're killing me," he moaned.

Unable to stand any more of her sweet torture, Mitch pulled away for just a moment and leaned down to grab the box off the bed. Kelsey followed him, pressing kisses on his chest, scraping her teeth against his nipples while she dug into his thighs with her fingertips. Mitch pulled a condom from the package, fumbling with it, unable to get the damned thing open under her relentless caresses.

Taking it from him, Kelsey tore open the packet with a sultry smile. She pushed his hand aside when he tried to take over, and slid the condom over his turgid flesh, ever so slowly, until he thought he couldn't take another moment of not being inside her.

Picking her up with one smooth motion, he again pulled her legs around his waist, cradling her bottom in his hands. She moved slightly to position herself, and then lowered onto him, sliding over him with her exquisite warmth.

Kelsey took him inside her slowly. For all her frantic need, she wanted to savor his penetration, loving the feel of him as he gradually filled her, making her his. When he was fully sheathed in her body, she remained motionless, closed her eyes and threw her head back as she welcomed his possession.

"Tell me I'm not dreaming, Mitch," she whispered.

He didn't open his eyes as he responded thickly, "This is no dream, sweetheart. We're finally where we belong."

Mitch didn't speak anymore, and Kelsey didn't either. They didn't remain still for long. Mitch's hands were at her hips and he pulled her against him as he began to move. Kelsey caught his rhythm, matched it, positively danced to it. Growing mindless as she met his every thrust, she felt the room begin to spin and became dizzy, thinking surely she could take no more.

Then all the sensations coursing through her body centered somewhere deep within her and began exploding, over and over until she screamed with the sheer rapture of it. Mitch's groan of satisfaction joined hers and together, still joined, they collapsed onto the bed.

A DELICIOUS MOIST WARMTH tickled the back of Kelsey's knee, and she stretched and extended her leg. She was only slightly awake. The ticklish feeling slowly moved up the back of her thigh, and she shivered, both with the pleasure of it and from the chilly air touching her skin. Gradually, languorously, she came more fully awake and noticed the pillowcase beneath her cheek was a smooth percale, not the flannel she was accustomed to. Of course, she remembered, she was in Mitch's bed. Remaining motionless, she sighed and enjoyed the feel of his mouth pressing kisses along her thigh.

"You're awake, aren't you?" he whispered against her skin, his stubbled flesh brushing against her and making her tingle.

"Uh-huh," she said with a sigh. "What time is it?"

It was still very dark in the room, the only light coming from the green neon bedside clock, which flashed twelve o'clock in annoying repetition.

"I have no idea," he said as he moved his mouth to her hip. "Do you care?"

"Not particularly," she replied.

Rolling over onto her back, Kelsey held her arms out for him, but Mitch would not be rushed. He took his own sweet time running his mouth across her flat belly. His exhalations flowed gently across her flesh, making her shiver more. He kissed his way up her body, inch by agonizing inch, skirting the areas she knew would make her go wild, as if he wanted to tantalize her for as long as possible before ending the wonderful torture. Kelsey was a quivering mass of nerve endings by the time he finally reached her face and began pressing light kisses on her jaw.

"Please..." she urged, not sure what she was asking for.

He continued his gentle assault. His hands were in motion now, stroking her thighs, her hips, her belly, still going nowhere near the pulsing core of her. She knew when he finally did touch her there, she would come apart all over again, and she writhed beneath him, nearly mindless.

Unable to resist, Kelsey began a reciprocal study of Mitch's body. He was hard, with long, muscular planes that she stroked and kneaded. Her fingertips danced across his supple skin, savoring the textures. He was ticklish at the ribs, sighed when she stroked his back, and hissed when she lightly bit his earlobe.

"Slow and steady this time, sweetheart," he whispered before dropping his mouth to hers for a long, slow, wet kiss.

Mitch could feel Kelsey shaking with her need. She was so beautifully responsive, arching into his hands, soundlessly pleading with him to bring her the release she craved. And finally he complied, sliding his hand down her body in one long, smooth caress and finding her heat.

Her heightened nerve endings exploded when he made his touch more intimate, and bolts of pleasure rocked through her instantly. She didn't even have time to come floating back to earth and suddenly he was sliding into her, building the pleasure all over again.

The loving was gentle and tender and so emotionally fulfilling that Kelsey nearly cried with the beauty of it.

THE PHONE WAS RIGHT by her ear and jarred Kelsey awake with its strident bellow. Not opening her eyes, she reached over to the bedside table and felt around until she found the receiver.

"Hello?" she muttered, still not fully awake.

"Kelsey?" came the surprised response.

"Mom?" she muttered, finally opening her eyes and glancing at the phone. It wasn't hers. Her phone was white and streamlined, and this one was black and bulky. She sat up in bed, staring wide-eyed around the room, with its mahogany furnishings and burgundy bedding, and at the dark man who stirred in the bed next to her. *Oh my God!*

Mitch, not really awake either, was about to answer the phone when the intrusive summons stopped in mid-ring. He rolled over and prepared to go back to sleep. Then he heard Kelsey's scratchy voice, saying hello and calling someone "mom." *Mom?* He bolted up.

"Oh, no, Mom…yeah, you probably misdialed," Kelsey said breathlessly, shooting Mitch an apologetic look. "No, that's okay. What time is it? No, the electricity went out last night and my clock's not working. Eight-thirty? No, that's fine, honestly."

Mitch ran his fingers through his mussed hair and listened to Kelsey's side of the conversation. He could not believe she had answered the phone, and, of all times, it was her mother calling! Marge Logan had only called twice in the past several weeks, and never this early on a Sunday morning.

Kelsey finished the call quickly and hung up the phone. She looked at him, biting her lip uncertainly. "Mitch, I'm sorry. I just wasn't thinking."

"What did she say?"

"She thought she dialed the wrong number. I imagine she'll be calling you back shortly."

Kelsey watched him frown. She couldn't stand to see the look of guilt on his face. She quickly reached to a chair next to the bed and grabbed the shirt he'd worn to the ball the night before. She slipped it over her head just as the phone rang. No way did she want to stick around and watch Mitch close up on her again, overcome with guilt while he talked to her mother. Not after last night. She got up and rushed to the bathroom.

"Hello?" she heard him answer before she shut the door with a click.

Kelsey studied her face in the bathroom mirror. Her makeup, which she'd neglected to take off the night before, was smeared on her face, and her hair was a wild, tangled mess. Her lips were swollen, so well kissed she didn't know if she'd ever stop feeling his mouth was still on hers.

"Of all the rotten timing," she muttered.

They should have been slowly waking up together, touching each other, sharing gentle kisses. There should have been that brief moment of embarrassment when they saw each other unclothed in the bright light of day. They ought to have had a long morning of loving to overcome any last vestiges of that embarrassment.

But that wasn't going to happen.

MITCH SAT IN THE MIDDLE of his bed after hanging up the phone, shocked at the conversation he'd just had with Marge Logan. Kelsey walked back in the room, her face a little cleaner, her hair combed down. She bit her lip uncertainly and held her hands behind her back. She wore his white blousy pirate shirt, and nothing else. His heart pounded harder in his chest and his mouth went dry. All she needed was a pair of high heels and she'd look like every man's number one fantasy.

And she was his.

"You know, your mother is one smart woman."

Kelsey slowly approached the far corner of the bed and gingerly sat down, not saying a word.

"I answered, and the first words out of her mouth were 'I hit the redial.'"

Kelsey groaned. "What did you say?"

"What do you think I said? I told her the truth. I've never lied to your parents and I'm sure as hell not going to start now."

Mitch watched her eyes widen, thoroughly enjoying the thought that for once *she* was the one who was speechless. He let her stew for a minute, then asked, "Has *everyone* known that you've been crazy about me for years?"

"What?" she screeched, jerking back so hard that she slid off the silky sheet and fell from the bed with a loud thump.

He jumped up, ran around the bed to see if she was

all right, and found her laughing on the hard floor. He started laughing too, as he reached to help her up.

"She said your father and your brothers have been placing bets on how long it would take you to get what you wanted...namely, me."

Kelsey didn't know what to say. The oh-so-rigid college professor should have been in the middle of a panic attack. But this Mitch...oh, this was the Mitch of her dreams, the Mitch of last night. His eyes sparkled, and a huge grin creased his lips.

"What exactly did you tell my mother?"

"Exactly? I'm not sure of the exact words. But I let her know that little Kelsey had finally roped herself a man."

Kelsey grabbed a pillow off the bed and smacked him in the head with it. He held up his hands protectively in front of himself, laughing as he fell back on the bed.

"Well, maybe I was a *little* more tactful," he admitted as she advanced on him threateningly with the pillow. He grinned and slid farther back until he'd reached the top end of the bed. "I told her we weren't sure what was happening between us yet, and she very gracefully told me she'd mind her own business. I didn't come right out and proclaim we're lovers."

Lovers. She liked that word on his lips. And she positively adored that he didn't mind saying it. The fact that her parents understood helped tremendously. Of course, that would probably only hold true as long as they believed Mitch and Kelsey were going to be married. And Kelsey didn't imagine Mitch had started thinking that far ahead yet. But Kelsey had. She'd fantasized about it for years. She'd fooled herself into thinking she suffered only from a major attraction for

Mitch. But the truth was, she'd been in love with him for a very long time. Now, in the morning, in his bed, still feeling warm and drowsy and slightly tender from their delicious intimacy, she could admit that to herself. But she didn't think he was quite ready to hear it. She'd give him a little while to get used to the whole situation.

Mitch couldn't believe how his life had changed in the past twelve hours. Only last night he'd been telling himself that getting involved with Kelsey would betray her family. Now, not only had he experienced the most erotically pleasurable night of his life, but he'd gotten her family's tentative blessing, as well. Mitch chuckled out loud, still marveling at how perceptive Kelsey's mother was. She'd come right out and told him she'd wanted them to be together for years, that she and Ralph had decided long ago that Mitch and Kelsey made the perfect couple.

It seemed he was the only one who'd had trouble coming to that realization. Remembering the night before, he knew he'd never regret it. In the dark, stormy depths of the night, coming together with Kelsey had been as elemental as the weather. He hadn't questioned it, hadn't second-guessed it, and had loved every minute of it.

"Last night was amazing," he said.

She smiled gently, admitting, "I thought so, too. I never imagined...I mean, Lady Love might sound like she knows everything, but to tell you the truth, Mitch, I never knew such feelings were possible. I didn't know something could be so pleasurable, so totally mind-consuming. I've been wanting to make love with you for the longest time, but until last night, I didn't even know what making love really was."

Mitch noted that nothing was as arousing to a man as knowing how completely he satisfied his woman. And at that moment Kelsey looked like a well-contented cat who'd licked clean a huge bowl of rich cream. His body responded instantly.

"So, we've given in to this incredible attraction that's been building for weeks," he said softly. "What now?"

"Well," she said playfully, sliding his shirt off her shoulders and letting it fall to the floor, "we could give in again."

Her green eyes narrowed and she crawled toward him from the foot of the bed. Mitch crawled to meet her halfway.

10

"I WANT TO TELL YOU MY FANTASIES."

Kelsey leaned closer to the microphone, dropping her voice to a sultry whisper. "Those delightful little vignettes we imagine, those interludes we allow ourselves to dwell on for brief moments during our day, or for long hours at night, are our fantasies. Those scenes we picture as we're slowly waking from a long night of evocative or haunting dreams. They taunt us, floating in the outer reaches of our minds, and we sometimes don't even remember them when we are fully awake. But they're there, waiting to visit us again, waiting to tantalize us with their seductive promise when we are ready to surrender our minds to them."

"DAMN!" MITCH MUTTERED as he stared in frustration at his gray slacks, which he'd just coated with half a can of spray starch. Kelsey's voice and words had completely distracted him. He'd been standing in his living room late Monday night, figuring he'd do some ironing while he listened to her show. He planned to wait up for her. He'd hated to watch her leave earlier that evening. They'd been inseparable since Saturday night.

Glancing at the slacks, he realized there was no point in even trying to continue ironing. He'd have to wash the pants again, anyway, unless he wanted to walk around as stiff legged as a flamingo.

When Kelsey broke away for her first set of commercials, Mitch unplugged the iron, turned down the lights and sat heavily on the couch. He took a sip of his drink and settled back. He could not even try to do anything else but listen to her, whispering to him in the dark.

"FANTASIES COME IN MANY FORMS. There are wishes for the future that masquerade as fantasies. For instance, I fantasize that *Night Whispers* goes into syndication and gets picked up nationwide."

Kelsey laughed softly, inviting her listeners to laugh with her.

"I also fantasize about my personal life, who I might end up with, how he'll love me more then I ever thought anyone could. How we'll want to give up our individual lives to create a new one together, perhaps sharing that new life with children."

A sudden image of Mitch holding a sweet, dark-haired girl intruded, but Kelsey pushed it aside and continued.

"We fantasize about winning the lottery, about being discovered as a great artist, about writing a best-selling book. And all of these fantasies are important, and enriching."

Kelsey gave a low, throaty chuckle, knowing her audience knew her too well to think she was going to talk about *those* types of fantasies on her show.

"However, since this *is Night Whispers*, I think we'll talk about fantasies that are a little more...seductive."

"OH, MAN," MITCH SAID ALOUD at Kelsey's words. It was going to be a late night.

It was getting a little warm in his apartment, and he stripped off his sweatshirt, then reclined on the couch again, moving quietly as he tried to catch all of her words. And he made a deal with himself. For the next few hours, he was going to forget that the woman he was involved with was telling all of Baltimore about her most sensual fantasies. For tonight he'd just listen to Lady Love, knowing that when *Night Whispers* was over, Kelsey would be coming home to *him*.

"SINCE IT'S MY SHOW," she continued, "I get to go first, all right? And a little later, I'll open up the phones to you, my faithful listeners."

Kelsey and Brian had already decided that these calls would need to be screened very carefully. She didn't want the FCC sanctioning her show because some caller went over the top.

"First of all, I fantasize about being carried. I don't mean carried away, as in dazzled with romantic gestures, although that would be nice, too. I mean, physically carried. I am all for equal rights, but just once, I want a man to demonstrate that he's bigger and stronger than I am, sweep me off my feet and carry me away. Of course, it has to be the right man—and the right moment."

Brian made a gesture from the other side of the booth, then simulated a man wearing nothing but a towel. Kelsey grinned a secretive grin, remembering how Mitch had carried her Saturday night, first to the car, and later straight up the basement stairs into ecstasy.

"In one of my fantasies, this strong man sweeps me

in his arms and carries me out of a torrential storm. He kisses me with every step, rain sliding down our faces to our mouths, and his sopping hair brushing my cheek," she murmured, closing her eyes as the fantasy filled her mind. "The wind drives us toward shelter, and lightning fills the dark sky while thunder crashes all around us. When we reach a secluded cabin, he ever so gently pulls my wet clothing off my quivering body and draws me down to the floor where he warms me with his naked flesh."

Kelsey drew in a deep breath, silently urging her listeners to stick with her, then slowly released it.

"Gee, it's a little warm in here tonight," she said with a throaty laugh. "I think we'll take a short break and when we come back, I want to hear from you. Call me. Tell me your fantasies. Ladies, listen to our male callers, and gentlemen, perhaps you can get some ideas of what your women want. Don't leave me now. This is Lady Love on WAJO and I'll be back in a moment."

MITCH REMAINED in his living room during the entire show. He refilled his drink once, during a commercial, and turned down the thermostat a little as the room continued to feel warmer and warmer. His eyes growing heavy in the dark, he closed them and lay back to listen to Kelsey.

Her callers were inventive, amusing, some a little silly. Kelsey handled them all with grace and good humor, encouraging and rewarding their creativity but quick to interrupt any caller who tried to get too graphic, or the ones who tried to invent fantasies involving Lady Love. He had to admit she was good at her job. Very good. Throughout the show, Kelsey never lost control. Those who didn't know Lady Love might think she was just enjoying herself, letting the conversation take her where it might, but Mitch knew her better. He recognized the deliberate pauses, the breathy sighs. Kelsey was polished and professional and seductive as hell.

She read a passage from *Lady Chatterley's Lover*, her voice lovingly caressing the torrid words. And then she played a torchy Tina Turner song about a dancer for hire. The two shouldn't have gone together, but somehow they did.

A lonely-sounding man talked about how much he fantasized meeting someone like his mother, then another spoke of female cops in bikinis. Kelsey helped one woman build on a scenario involving a closed theme park and a certain superhero character, and Mitch laughed until tears came out of his eyes at the story they concocted.

But her own fantasies held him utterly enthralled. She liked strawberries and chocolate. He hadn't known that about her. She wanted to wake up on a bed of flower petals. That he could have guessed. She sometimes imagined she was a romance novel heroine and a tall, strong man swept her up on a horse and they rode on a beach, along a rough, rocky shore all night long.

She wanted to make love on a staircase.

When he heard that one, Mitch remembered their first heated kisses on the stairs and groaned out loud. He wanted Kelsey so badly that he physically ached.

"So, MY FRIENDS, we're coming to the end of another *Night Whispers*. Not a bad way to spend a Monday evening, was it? I hope you got a little inspiration. I know I did. I thank you for your ideas and your calls. Those of you who couldn't get through, please don't give up. We will have many other interesting topics to discuss in all those long nights to come."

Brian rolled his arm forward, letting her know she had a little more time to fill, so Kelsey continued.

"Here's one final little secret fantasy I'll share. I fantasize that one day a certain incredibly sexy man will take off the blinders he's wearing over those gorgeous velvety blue eyes of his and admit he's madly in love with me."

Kelsey paused, then delivered the punch line.

"Of course, I guess Mel Gibson's wife would have something to say about that!"

Brian shook his finger at her playfully through the glass, telling her he knew exactly whose blue eyes she'd been talking about.

"Again, thank you all. You've been listening to *Night Whispers*, with Lady Love, here on WAJO. Please come visit me tomorrow. I'll be waiting."

A HALF HOUR LATER, Brian and Kelsey picked up their things and prepared to leave the break room.

"Great show," he said again. "I have to say, Lady Love was especially sultry tonight. Any particular reason?"

She shrugged her shoulders and feigned ignorance. "Not a clue."

He laughed out loud and held the door open for her. "Looks like Mr. Faithful's on duty tonight. Tell me, has he worked up the nerve to ask you out yet?" Brian murmured as they walked into the lobby and he nodded toward the station doors.

Kelsey followed his glance and saw Edgar, the station's full-time security guard. She was glad he was the one on duty. "Don't be silly. He's just a very nice man...a very nice *married* man."

Brian sighed. "Honey, that doesn't stop some men."

"Well, I guarantee it would stop him. I met his wife one evening when she brought him his dinner. She definitely wears the pants in that family."

Kelsey smiled as they reached the guard at the door. Edgar was quiet, unassuming, almost bookish. At first she'd been a little unsure of his qualifications as a guard, but she'd heard he was very coolheaded, and good with his gun. He seemed devoted to her, and was always respectful and polite.

"And better him than Charlie," she muttered after Edgar stepped outside to glance around the parking lot before ushering them out.

"That meathead?" Brian scoffed. "Yeah, I guess you're right. Edgar might not look intimidating, but at least he looks intelligent. Charlie, on the other hand, looks like a slab of human muscle without an ounce of brainpower."

If it was just the lack of intelligence, Kelsey might not have minded Charlie, the other regular guard, so much. The man was good-looking, tall, broad, blond and confident. But he had made several comments to her about how he could help her with *Night Whispers*. His flirtatiousness made her uncomfortable. She much preferred Edgar.

"Ready, Miss Logan?" Edgar asked as he stepped back inside and gave them an all-clear sign.

She nodded, and the two men escorted her to her car.

MITCH STOOD OUTSIDE his apartment door, watching from the foyer window for Kelsey. It was forty-five minutes after her show ended, and he knew she'd be arriving home at any minute. He hadn't told her he'd wait up for her and wondered if her first instinct would be to go up to her apartment or to come to him. It didn't matter. He wasn't going to give her a choice.

She arrived moments later, and he grinned as he leaned back in the dark, waiting for her. What a change from the first time he'd waited up after one of Lady Love's performances. Now he wasn't going to kiss her to shut her up. He was going to kiss her to make her moan in ecstasy.

Kelsey entered the dark brownstone, locked the front door behind her and reached her hand toward Mitch's door. Before she could grasp the knob, a hand closed around her wrist. She screamed.

"Kelsey, baby, it's only me!" Mitch said.

Her heart pounded a mile a minute and Kelsey raised a shaking hand to her face. "Would you stop doing that?" she shouted. "You scared the heck out of me again!"

"I'm sorry, sweetheart, really. I was just trying to surprise you. What's wrong? Did something happen?"

"No, I'm fine, you just startled me. I'm tired. For some reason I didn't get much sleep the past couple of nights," she said, now smiling crookedly.

Mitch opened the door and led her into his apartment. He slid her coat off her shoulders and tossed it onto the couch, then gently rubbed the tense muscles on the sides of her neck.

"Sorry to disappoint you, sweetheart, but you ain't gonna get much sleep tonight, either. At least not for a while."

He kissed the sensitive spot of skin where her neck met her shoulders, and Kelsey instantly felt the tension drain from her body. It was replaced by heat, anticipation, desire. All the feelings Mitch's touch aroused.

He was right. She didn't get to sleep for a long, long time.

IN THE DAYS THAT FOLLOWED, Kelsey was happier than she had ever thought possible. Mitch was attentive and adoring, incredibly romantic and thoughtful. Each night when she got home from work, she'd find him waiting in the well-lit foyer to sweep her into his apartment. She never took for granted that he'd be waiting, not wanting to upset the perfect balance their relationship had reached. But he was always there.

He fulfilled her every desire. One night she came home from work and found his bed covered with rose petals. A bowl of red strawberries and a fondue pot with melted chocolate sat on the table.

"You heard my show on fantasies, didn't you!"

"Guilty," he said as he dipped a juicy berry into the chocolate and held it to her mouth.

She bit into the succulent fruit, licking the chocolate that dripped down his fingers. "Lady Love can be pretty useful, can't she?"

"I try to forget that you and Lady Love are the same person. But I have to admit, she does have some terrific ideas."

"She's got great inspiration."

Mitch pulled away for a moment and frowned. "Kelsey, what happens here is just for us, all right? I would hate it if you ever brought our personal life onto the air with you."

"Don't worry," she said. "Gee, it's awfully warm in here tonight." Kelsey unbuttoned her slacks and wiggled out of them, sliding them to her feet as slowly as she could. Mitch watched her every move, and she pretended she didn't notice his eyes darken and his breath come more quickly.

He knew she was trying to change the subject, and allowed her to succeed. While Kelsey sat back down on the bed next to him, Mitch dipped another berry for her. As he lifted it to her mouth, he accidentally dripped a thick drop of chocolate onto her bare thigh. Pushing her back onto the pillows, Mitch slowly and thoroughly licked the sweet candy away. After that, the dripping chocolate was anything but accidental.

Lady Love's fantasies didn't compare with the reality of Kelsey's nights.

HER DAYS WEREN'T BAD, either. When they weren't making love, Kelsey was doing her best to make Mitch misbehave. She loved teasing him in the middle of his research, shocking that studious look off his face by cranking up the stereo and dancing around his living room. She liked that he'd drop his work to take her out to see a stupid movie just because she asked him to. The fact that the movie stank and he enthusiastically threw popcorn at the screen with her made it that much better.

So far, the only bone of contention between them was her job.

"Mitch, we've been over this," Kelsey said one afternoon as they sorted laundry in the basement. "You said yourself I'm doing a great job and that *Night Whispers* is a terrific show."

"Yeah, it's a terrific show. If anyone else were Lady

Love, I'm sure I'd be perfectly happy to lie in bed with you some nights, letting her inspire us."

"I don't think we need it," Kelsey said with a sly grin.

"True," he conceded with masculine vanity. "Still, you get my point. I worry about you. Kelsey, you're appealing to people's innermost passion. You're their fantasy woman, their sexual dream come to life. There are a lot of men out there who won't be able to separate Lady Love the character from you, *my* woman."

"Your woman? Ooh, you sound so caveman. I like it, I like it," she said, trying to change the subject and make him laugh. It didn't work.

"Look, Lady Love makes me so hot I think I'm going to crawl out of my own skin," he said. "But, baby, it bothers me knowing that a lot of other men in this city feel the same way."

Kelsey sighed and tossed a load of her jeans into the dryer. Mitch was right next to her, leaning back against the washer, with his arms folded across his chest.

"But I come home to you," she said. "The only one who makes Lady Love feel hot enough to crawl out of her skin is the man I'm looking at. And, my, you are certainly fine to look at, Mitch Wymore."

Mitch saw the heat in her gaze as she ran her eyes over his body with the intensity of a touch. He'd come to recognize her physical responses, and knew by the way she bit her bottom lip that her mind was conjuring up a multitude of pleasures. Finding a few flooding his own mind, he forgot about her job.

Never taking his eyes from her, he reached behind his back and started the washing machine. She hadn't put any clothes in it. Sudden understanding lit her face. Her lips curled into a sultry smile as he pulled her closer and let her feel his body's hot reaction to her.

"What is it with you and basements?" she asked breathily.

He answered by slowly lifting his shirt over his head and tossing it aside. The cold air didn't deter him in the least; in fact, it exhilarated him. Almost as much as she did.

She ran her fingertips from the top of one shoulder down across his chest and stomach to the waistband of his pants. He let her undress him, closing his eyes and stifling a groan as she slowly pushed his jeans down with her flat palms.

When he moved to unbutton her blouse, she took a step back with a seductive smile. Never saying a word, she slowly stripped her clothes off, piece by piece. He watched her every movement, building the desire and heat by touching her with nothing but his eyes.

Finally he reached out one hand and curled it around her naked hip. He pulled her against him. Trailing kisses on her jaw, he licked the side of her neck, then scraped his teeth on her earlobe. She shivered in his arms. He knew it wasn't from the cold. She pressed hard against him, silently demanding what she wanted.

"Spin or rinse?" he whispered, then couldn't form another thought.

THE NEXT EVENING Kelsey sat in an office she used at the station, reviewing some notes. *Night Whispers* was doing very well—the ratings proved it. She was going to try to make sure it stayed that way.

"I hear you got some flowers today," Brian said as he entered the office, "from your knight."

Kelsey bit her lip, not wanting to get into another discussion with Brian about her secret admirer. But the man knew everything that happened around the station. No way would the delivery of a dozen red roses escape his notice.

"Yeah. They were delivered this afternoon."

"And you still think this person is just doing a little harmless letter writing? Sounds to me like he's getting a little more serious. What does Mitch think about it?"

Kelsey bit the corner of her lip and averted her eyes, saying, "He doesn't exactly know."

"Not *exactly*? What, *exactly*, have you told him?"

Kelsey defiantly replied, "None of it."

Seeing he was about to argue with her, she held up her hands to stop him. "Look, Brian, Mitch isn't thrilled about *Night Whispers* as it is. He's concerned about me enough and I certainly don't want to give him any more reason to worry."

"You're an idiot."

She scowled at him.

"I mean it," Brian said, not letting up on her one bit. "Don't you know lying like this is bound to come back around and bite you in the rear sooner or later?"

"I'm not lying."

"Deceiving by omission, then."

"Look," Kelsey explained, "Mitch has a lot on his plate right now. He's receiving a special award for those wonderful newspaper articles he wrote while he was in China. It means a lot of exposure and could really help him with his writing. The last thing he needs is to worry about me."

Kelsey stood to leave the room and Brian followed.

"Promise me something, all right? If anything else happens, you'll tell him about it."

She didn't want to. Kelsey knew full well how Mitch would react. He'd envision an entire stalker scenario and have her carrying mace and a stun gun. But she knew Brian was right.

"I will. *After* the awards banquet. Now, can we please focus on the show we have to start in just about four minutes?"

He nodded and fell into step beside her as she walked to the studio. "You have your opening?"

"Uh-huh," Kelsey said with a nod. "Did you put the CDs in order for me?"

"All done. Sounds like it's going to be very romantic."

"I hope so," she said. "I definitely hope so."

Mitch turned on the radio a few minutes before Kelsey's show came on, listening for her intro while he made himself a quick ham sandwich in the kitchen. When he heard the saxophone music start, he grabbed a drink and rushed into the living room.

"Hello, Baltimore, this is Lady Love and you're listening to *Night Whispers* on WAJO. I think the time has come, dear friends, to talk about love."

Mitch dropped his sandwich and had to quickly wipe a spot of mustard off the leather sofa. Lady Love was going to talk about love? He'd never heard her on that topic before. Usually she focused on the more physical side of relationships, not the emotional.

"*Love* is a word bandied about all the time in our daily lives. I love my new red dress, and I just love Brad Pitt's latest movie, and oh, how I love spicy Mexican food."

Mitch wondered if she was going to talk about other

things she "loved." Like how she loved having that tender strip of skin at the very top of her thigh lightly bitten. He didn't think she would; after all, he'd made himself very clear about how he felt about her bringing their private relationship onto the air.

"We use the word *love* lightly when we talk about people, too. We just love our favorite sports figure, or a great teacher. The word only begins to reflect its true meaning, however, when we're speaking about people for whom we have deep, lasting emotions."

Relieved she wasn't going to go into further detail about what she loved, Mitch settled back on the sofa to listen.

"I suppose the first love we experience as human beings is the love of our parents. A mother who takes her squalling, red-faced, newborn bundle into her arms doesn't see the blotches—she sees perfection. She loves this creature because she has created it, and it is a part of her. As children, we respond to that love, blooming into little people under the constant tender care and emotional sustenance. And we love our siblings and other family members who weave like a tight tapestry into our developing lives."

Kelsey would be a great mother. Mitch didn't know where the thought came from, but he knew it was true.

"Then, of course, there's romantic love."

Ahh! Now we get to it! Mitch smiled wryly as Kelsey segued into the topic he knew she was planning.

"When we're teenagers, our hormones tell us we're in love before we even fully comprehend what that word means. Then, one day, we finally get it. We finally realize what love really is. Now, this might not happen until we hit sixty, but hey, I firmly believe it will happen to every person at least once. Real love. Not lust, not compatibility, but real love."

Kelsey's voice trailed off, and Mitch heard music. The song asked for just one minute of "real love." When she returned to the air, after the song and a commercial break, Kelsey picked up where she'd left off.

"Now, about real love...I want to hear from all of you about when you discovered it existed. I want to know the exact moment the excitement you felt when he walked into the room turned into absolute devastation when he left it. Gentlemen, don't be shy tonight. I want to know when you realized the woman you asked out to dinner became the woman you wanted to spend your life with."

Mitch wondered if she knew he was listening. Was she asking him to evaluate his feelings for her? Mitch wasn't ready to do that, but she seemed to be forcing the issue.

"Your physical attraction to him, the excitement you feel when you're in his arms, that's only the beginning. It's also your complete trust in him, knowing he'll be on your side even if you've done something totally stupid, the idea that you'd rather stay home with him to watch an old movie than get dolled up and go out. These are clues of love. Realizing that he doesn't care if you look like Frankenstein's bride the morning after a party, or that he'll tell you your bathing suit looks terrific even if you know you look fat in it, looking at him doing something as simple as reading a newspaper and thinking just how much you actually *like* him...well, now you're in very deep."

Mitch smiled during her brief pause. He liked her, too.

She continued. "Now, add that moment when you're ready to scream because he left the toilet seat up and then he hands you a bunch of flowers he picked from your own garden. Your annoyance just evaporates. That's the moment. Real love is when all the varied feelings you have for another person come together in an instant of utter clarity and you realize your life was a huge empty shell before he stepped into it."

Mitch frowned. This was just a show. Kelsey was onstage when she did *Night Whispers*. She spoke about topics designed to encourage callers and help her ratings. So why did he feel she was reaching through the speakers, telling him, and only him, how she felt?

"Real love…once you find it, hold it tight and never take it for granted. It will last if you nurture it. And when you are both old and gray and slow in your movements and have only each other to laugh at your bad jokes, it will still be there."

As a song began to play, Mitch walked to the stereo to turn it off. He didn't want to hear any more.

Mitch paced around the living room, nearly tripping over a pair of shoes she'd left on the floor near the fireplace. One soft leather glove lay near the door. A fashion magazine rested on the coffee table among the archaeological journals, and a bottle of pale pink nail polish stood on an end table. The room was filled with her light scent. He couldn't turn around without seeing something that belonged to her or reminded him of her.

When had he fallen in love with her? For there was no question that he loved her. Her words tonight had forced him to acknowledge that. He'd reached that "moment" she'd been babbling on about and now didn't know what on earth to do about it.

He couldn't love Kelsey. He liked her. He was amazingly attracted to her. He'd drifted into an affair with her against all common sense. But he didn't have room in his life to love her.

Mitch was essentially a loner, getting mentally swept away when studying something that intrigued him. He'd never planned on marrying and raising a family. He liked being able to pick up and leave the country for six months at a time. He liked his calm, unencumbered life.

With Kelsey, he found his emotions called the shots and his brain ran to catch up. She appealed to a part of him he thought he'd managed to suppress, the part of him that didn't fit in with his current existence.

Using every bit of his analytical experience, Mitch went over and over the reasons he couldn't love Kelsey. A couple of hours later, he nearly had himself convinced.

But, of course, when she walked in the door and smiled that smile, he knew he was a goner.

11

KELSEY DIDN'T THINK too much about the roses. After all, they'd arrived at the station, just as the letters had. The address was right in the phone book for anyone to see.

The balloons in her car were another matter entirely. Brian and Edgar both noticed them right away as they walked her out after her show the following night.

"You going to a birthday party or something?" Brian asked.

"I have no idea where they came from," Kelsey said softly as she opened the door and retrieved the huge bouquet. The balloons were brightly colored, with swirling ribbons attached. Holding the ribbons together at the bottom was a chess piece. A white knight.

"Subtle," Brian said with a smirk.

"Pretty," murmured Edgar.

"Goodbye," said Kelsey as she yanked the knight off and let go of the ribbons. The balloon bouquet flew up out of her hands and was picked up by a breeze that carried it over the city. She didn't say another word as she got in her car—which she knew she occasionally forgot to lock—and left the parking lot. Kelsey tried hard not to think about the fact that someone had actually come to the station and, knowing which car was hers, had gotten into it while she was inside the building.

Luckily, Mitch helped her forget when she got home that night.

THEY SLEPT LATE the next morning, as they usually did on weekdays. Mitch had adjusted his sleep schedule to fit in with Kelsey's work hours and enjoyed waking up slowly beside her every midmorning.

"I wish you'd change your mind and let me come to the banquet with you tomorrow night," she said as she snuggled close to him. "Baltimore can survive one night without Lady Love if I call in sick."

"You'd be bored stiff. I'm not looking forward to going, myself."

Kelsey sat up and stretched. Since she slept naked, Mitch couldn't help pausing to admire the picture she made. He felt his body harden in instant response.

"You should be thrilled about it," she said. "You're being honored by a charitable organization for some very wonderful work you did. Foreign adoption agencies in the city have really benefited from those articles you wrote last summer."

"I'm proud of the award, Kels, just not too interested in being around the Downtown Charitable Society. I know some of the members. Rich snobs who dabble in good works. Believe me, tomorrow night will be a bore. I'd be just as pleased to accept the plaque in my own living room."

Mitch saw her nibble at her lip and glance away. He sensed there was something she wasn't saying. "What's wrong?"

"I just wondered, I mean, it's not that you don't *want* me there, is it? I mean, I don't imagine it would do your reputation a lot of good to show up with the infamous Lady Love on your arm."

Hearing the uncertain tone in her voice, Mitch immediately sat up and drew her into his arms. He was shocked that she would even think he could somehow be ashamed of her. "Kelsey, you're crazy. The problems I have with your job have absolutely nothing to do with embarrassment or worry about my reputation. It's your safety that concerns me. I'd be the luckiest guy in the place if I showed up with you on my arm tomorrow night."

She nodded, reassured, and Mitch lay back against the pillows, pulling her down with him.

"Maybe I'll plan on giving you a private little award tomorrow night in your own living room," she offered in a sultry whisper.

"How about a preview?" he said with a grin.

Smiling, she slid on top of him and complied.

"WHAT HAPPENS WHEN attraction becomes obsession?"

Kelsey saw Brian's frown from the other side of the booth. She'd changed topics on him with no warning again.

"You and I have talked many times, my friends, about desire, about wanting someone. But we've never really discussed that line...that fine line between being attracted to someone and being obsessed with them. Tonight I want to talk about it. Call me. This is Lady Love and you're listening to *Night Whispers* on WAJO."

Kelsey sat back in her chair, confident about her decision to change tonight's topic. She didn't really feel like getting on the air and talking about the "funniest places people made love." Not after last night's balloon incident, and the love letter she'd received earlier today. In it, her admirer commented on how much he had liked the way she'd worn her hair one night last week. For the first time since the whole "knight" business had begun, she was actually feeling a little nervous. Somewhere, this man was watching her, paying attention to where she parked and what she looked like. It was a disconcerting feeling.

"I know how it feels to lie alone at night, dreaming about being with someone who doesn't feel the same way. It can physically hurt, wanting him that much. So you start to imagine he wants you, too. You fantasize, planning how perfect your relationship will be once you get his attention. But how far should you go to get that attention? Call me, tell me about it."

The show sped by quickly. *Night Whispers* was never short on callers. Dozens of people were anxious to talk about their own brushes with dangerous love.

"I never realized there were that many lonely, lovesick people in Baltimore," Brian muttered as he walked her to the lobby after the show ended.

"Yeah, but none of them sounded like my lonely, lovesick knight," Kelsey replied.

"You're lucky. That's the last thing you need, to get this guy on the air and fuel whatever sick fantasy he's got going."

Kelsey saw Edgar waiting for them. The guard unlocked the front doors as they approached. As they walked toward her car, she prayed there would not be a repeat of the balloon incident.

"Everything looks A-okay, Miss Logan," Edgar said as he held her driver's side door open for her while she got in.

"All right, then, I'm outta here," Brian said as he waved and hopped into his own car. He beeped as he quickly pulled away.

Kelsey waved back, then inserted her key into the ignition and turned it. Nothing happened. She tried again, pumping the gas pedal a few times, mentally cursing the sporty little coupe. Why could cars never break down in their own garages?

Edgar knocked on her car window, startling her as he asked, "Having some trouble?"

"It's just dead."

Kelsey stepped out of the car to allow Edgar to get in and try to start it. Nothing happened. He popped the hood and got out to look under it. Kelsey was glad the man seemed to know what he was doing, because she wouldn't have known a carburetor from a gas tank.

"I can't see what's wrong, Miss Logan. I think maybe you'll have to have it towed to a garage tomorrow."

She groaned.

"Hey, I'll let them know inside and I'll drive you home. It won't take me long."

"I can't put you out. I'll call a cab," Kelsey said.

"I wouldn't hear of it," he insisted. "We can't have some stranger coming and picking you up in the middle of the night. Keeping you safe is my job and I take it very seriously."

He puffed out his chest and hitched up the loose waist of his pants. Kelsey bit her lip to stop a grin. His bravado seemed so out of character in the small, balding, middle-aged man. She was suddenly reminded of Barney Fife from the old *Andy Griffith Show*.

"Okay, Edgar, I really would appreciate it."

She waited for him in the lobby while he got his keys and locked up the building for those remaining inside. When he was finished, he took her by the arm and led her back to the parking lot. As they neared his blue pickup truck, Kelsey noticed it sat in a very large, muddy puddle. It had rained earlier in the day, and Edgar had managed to park right in the middle of a huge, water-filled pothole.

She glanced ruefully at her brown leather shoes, hiked her pants up a bit and prepared to step into the water.

"Oh, no, Miss Logan, let me," Edgar protested.

Before she realized his intention, the man bent over and picked her up. He staggered under her weight. He stood only a few inches taller than she did.

Kelsey yelped. "Edgar, put me down!"

"Can't let you ruin your shoes," he panted as he sloshed through the water.

Edgar shifted her so she pressed against the side of the truck while he tried to open the door. She knew he was going to drop her about two seconds before he actually did it. Luckily, as his arms gave out, she leaned back and slid down the side of the truck, using it to keep her balance as her feet splashed into the muddy water.

Breathing a quick sigh of relief that she hadn't landed on her fanny on the pavement, she looked down at her sopping wet shoes.

"Oh, Miss Logan, I'm so sorry!"

"No, don't pick me up," she ordered when he moved to lift her again.

Edgar took a quick step back, losing his balance. Kelsey reached out to grab his arm, and he clutched at her hand, pulling her with him. They both went down,

Kelsey landing on her rear end right in the middle of the puddle.

Feeling cold water seep into the weave of her beige slacks, Kelsey closed her eyes. She didn't know whether to burst into tears or shriek with laughter. Lifting her arms, she placed her elbows on her knees and dropped her head into her hands.

"Oh, please, don't cry, Miss Logan. I'll pay for your clothes to get clean."

She heard the misery in Edgar's voice, lifted her head and struggled to smile. The man looked utterly mortified.

"It's all right, Edgar. Why don't we just go now, okay?"

He insisted on helping her up. She climbed inside as he walked around to the driver's side door, his wet black boots making a squeaking, sloshing sound she could hear from inside the truck. Kelsey felt a grin tickle her lips. When he got inside the truck, he hung his head sheepishly and wouldn't meet her eyes.

"It's really all right, Edgar. I know you're just trying to help."

He glanced up, gave her a faltering smile and nodded. Kelsey held in a laugh when she saw a soggy leaf fall from his shoulder onto his lap. Shifting in her wet seat, she made herself as comfortable as possible for the ride home.

MITCH GLANCED AT THE CLOCK and frowned. Kelsey was late. She usually arrived home at around two forty-five and it was already past three. He couldn't help worrying. It was bad enough that her job was so provocative. The fact that she had to drive home alone in the middle of the night made it that much worse.

He saw headlights swing into the driveway and breathed a sigh of relief. He walked into the foyer just as Kelsey came in the front door.

"You're late," he said as he slid his arms around her waist and pulled her tightly against him. "I was getting worried. Hey, your pants are wet!"

"I'm sorry," she said breathlessly. "I had car trouble and had to get a ride home from someone. I slipped in a puddle. Klutz, huh?"

Mitch saw a car back out of the driveway and pull away up the street. "Who was that? Brian?"

"No, it was Edgar. I don't think you've met him."

"Edgar, hmm? Should I be jealous?"

Kelsey giggled. "Baby, you'd have no reason to be jealous if Leonardo DiCaprio drove me home. I am all yours."

He kissed her neck, liking her words. She was all his.

"Prove it," he challenged as he drew her into his living room.

"That sounds like an order," she murmured as she let her jacket fall off her shoulders onto the floor.

"I'd never dream of ordering you to do anything you didn't want to do," he said as he began sliding the buttons of her blouse open, one by one. Then he cocked a sly grin. "I prefer to use gentle persuasion."

He whispered a suggestion in her ear and heard her moan deep in her throat. She rolled her head to the side and let her blouse fall off her shoulders. Mitch followed the fine curve of her neck and shoulder with his tongue as he unzipped her slacks and let them slide, along with her underclothes, down her legs. He kissed a path down her body, pausing for a delectable moment or two to taste her breasts before dropping to his knees on the floor in front of her. He was glad he reached his arms behind her legs and held her thighs steady because when he began intimately caressing her with his mouth, her knees nearly buckled.

"Gentle persuasion works," she muttered while she was still somewhat coherent.

Mitch barely heard her.

SOMETHING WOKE HIM EARLY the following morning. Mitch glanced at Kelsey, sleeping soundly beside him, then saw the clock. It was just past eight. Very early, considering they hadn't gone to sleep until after four that morning. A languorous smile crossed his lips when he remembered how she'd kept him awake to try some gentle persuasion of her own after they'd moved to the bedroom. Lady Love's mouth was absolutely amazing even when she didn't say a word, he thought.

Mitch heard another noise coming from the front of the house.

Quickly getting out of bed, he pulled a pair of sweatpants over his naked body. He didn't know what the noise had been, maybe a car passing close to the house, possibly a horn blown nearby. But the creak had seemed close, and familiar.

Walking through the living room into the foyer, he saw a box and a piece of paper lying on the floor by the front door. He immediately realized what he'd heard creaking: the mail slot.

Kelsey realized she was alone when she started to feel cold. She shifted over in her sleep, seeking Mitch's warm body, but found his side of the bed empty. She sat up with a start.

"Mitch?"

He didn't answer. Curious, she got out of bed, slipped on one of his shirts over her head and walked toward the front of the house.

The door between the living room and foyer was slightly ajar. Kelsey walked to it and gingerly pushed it open. "Mitch? What's wrong?"

She saw him squatting in the foyer, holding a long, thin box covered with gold foil that looked as if it contained expensive candy. Mitch rose to his feet, staring steadily at her. He slowly extended his arm, offering her the box.

"Mitch? What is it?"

He narrowed his eyes and held out his other hand. Kelsey recognized the pale-blue-colored stationery he held. She winced.

"Who the hell is 'Your Knight'?"

Kelsey grimaced, then squared her shoulders. "Let's go sit down and I'll tell you all about it."

Mitch didn't appear to want to move, but finally he dropped the box and followed her into his living room.

After she'd told him the entire story, he stared at her in consternation for several seconds before speaking, "So, someone's been harassing you for weeks, and you never once even bothered to *mention* it to me?"

Kelsey ran a weary hand over her eyes. What she really wanted was a strong cup of coffee or a few more hours' sleep. He seemed intent on arguing. "Mitch, please, don't get upset."

"Upset?" he said with a bitter laugh. "That doesn't quite describe what I'm feeling, Kelsey."

She cringed.

He paced back and forth across the wood floor. His bare feet struck the surface hard enough to make thudding noises. "I'm angry and I'm hurt by this," he explained. Kelsey heard the emotion in his voice as he continued. "Why didn't you tell me? What on earth made you feel you couldn't trust me enough to share what you were going through?"

"Mitch, of course I trust you. I just didn't want to bother you with this."

"Bother me?" he replied as he stopped pacing and stared into her face, his eyes widening in disbelief. "You think telling me someone's stalking you is going to *bother* me? Good grief, Kelsey, I might be *bothered* if you said you didn't get a raise you wanted, or were concerned about your ratings. This goes way beyond *bothered!*"

Kelsey shrank back in her seat at the outright anger in his voice. She hadn't seen him this furious in a long time. She hated that she was the one who'd caused it.

"I thought you and I had something kind of meaningful building here," he muttered bitterly.

"We do!"

"Obviously, we don't," he retorted. "People in a relationship don't lie and keep secrets because they fear they'll *bother* the other person."

"I didn't lie."

"A technicality," he snapped. "Maybe you never came out and said, 'No, Mitch, no one has been writing me dozens of love letters, staking out the station and leaving me mystery gifts in my car,' but there were plenty of times when we talked about your job that you could have come clean. And you didn't. You kept your mouth shut, figuring I wouldn't like it and you didn't want to have to deal with that. Well, you know what? I *don't* like it, and you *do* have to deal with it!"

Kelsey took a deep breath and considered her words, wondering how she could make him understand. "Mitch, look, *bother* is the wrong word. It's just...I know how you feel about my job. I know you worry about me anyway. I didn't want to make you feel worse. Things are going so well for us—I wanted to keep it perfect for as long as possible."

He didn't soften one bit. "Gee, it really paid off, didn't it? Now on top of worrying about some wacko stalking you, I have to wonder if there's anything else going on that you haven't told me about because you want to 'keep things perfect' between us."

Kelsey bit her lip and shook her head vehemently. "No, Mitch. You know everything. And don't make it sound worse than it is. I'm not being stalked. It's not that terrible. I mean, I certainly don't feel threatened, just a little uncomfortable."

"You should feel threatened! What if when you opened your car door the other night you'd found some nut with a knife instead of just some balloons? He's been watching you, knows which one's your car, what you look like. And he has obviously followed you home, because he now knows where you live! That doesn't sound like normal behavior to me, Kelsey. Whoever's doing this has got a screw loose somewhere."

Mitch threw himself down in an armchair. Kelsey wished he'd sat beside her on the couch. She wanted him close. He obviously wanted some distance. She blinked rapidly to hold back tears.

"Mitch, I was wrong. I'm sorry. I should have come to you and told you about it. But can you honestly say that you would have been able to deal with it logically? To just sit back and wait for something to happen, for this guy to get caught or to stop? Because that's really all we can do."

"Hell, no," he retorted. "That's not all we can do. We can remove the temptation, not let Lady Love make Kelsey Logan a target for one more day."

Kelsey stood up and placed her hands on her hips, feeling anger replace the guilt she'd been feeling moments before. "What are you saying?"

Mitch stood and moved close to her until they were practically nose to nose. "What I'm saying is, no more *Night Whispers*, no more threat. Maybe even no more lies between us."

She crossed her arms across her chest and narrowed her eyes. "Did you just, basically, order me to quit my job? Because, for some reason, I seem to remember being in this room with you a few hours ago and hearing you say you'd never presume to order me to do anything."

Mitch's mouth tightened. "No, I'm not ordering you. I am relying on your common sense and your intelligence to make you come to the realization that quitting is the only answer."

Kelsey ground her teeth, hearing his college professor tone and not liking it one bit. "No, Mitch, quitting is not the only answer. Letting the police take care of this is one option, ignoring it is another, being extra vigilant is a third. These are other options...ones that I'm actually going to consider—unlike your suggestion, which I find totally ludicrous."

Kelsey saw Mitch stiffen, his face a cold, unfamiliar mask as he absorbed her words. She nearly regretted them, but forced herself to remember why she'd spit them out in the first place. He'd issued her an order, whether he saw it that way or not.

"So, you're not even going to discuss the possibility of quitting *Night Whispers*. Getting on the radio and sharing dirty little secrets with the lusting public is so important to you you'd risk your personal safety. And you'd throw away what you and I have."

She heard what he was really saying. Kelsey felt things spinning out of control. Their words were leading to heartache, but she couldn't do anything to stop them.

"And now it's not an order, it's an ultimatum? I quit or I lose you?" she asked, wanting to be sure she understood him correctly.

He didn't respond. She stood still for a few seconds, silently praying he'd take her in his arms and tell her they'd work through it together. He didn't move.

"You know, Mitch, maybe the real reason I didn't come to you with this whole 'knight' nonsense, is this. It's this moment. It's because I knew you'd use it as an excuse to try to convince me to give up something I love because it doesn't fit in with your ordered life."

Her voice broke and she felt tears falling from her eyes and down her cheeks. She angrily dashed them away with the back of her hand. "You're not just asking me to quit a job. You're asking me to be someone else, someone who walks away when threatened, who always plays it safe. I'm not that someone. Mitch, you fell into this relationship with me with your eyes wide-open. You knew who I was from day one, and I never tried to deny it. And deep down, beneath that safe, conservative shell of yours, I know damn well you don't want me to do what you're asking me to do."

Tears continued to fall down her cheeks and Kelsey didn't even bother wiping them away.

Mitch shook his head slowly. "You're wrong," he said with quiet dignity. "I'd be the happiest man alive if you never went back to that station. Don't you get it? I couldn't stand it if something happened to you."

Kelsey watched as he raised a weary hand to his brow and rubbed his temple. His movements were so familiar to her, she knew he'd swipe his hand through his hair the second before he did it. Her heart ached, but she could not back down.

"The worst thing that could happen to me," she explained softly, "is that I could allow someone else to dictate how I'll live my life. I will not change who I am to suit anyone. And if you don't know that about me, then you don't know me at all."

Mitch watched in silence as she strode toward the door. She paused, wrapping her arms around her body, as if gaining strength, then walked out of the apartment without another word.

He nearly went after her. Lots of things had been said before he'd even thought about what he was saying. The whole conversation should have been handled differently, when he wasn't so angry about the way he'd discovered what she'd been going through…and about the way she'd hidden it from him.

But he couldn't bring himself to follow her. Because he knew if he did they'd end up in each other's arms and he'd apologize and tell her he didn't mean it. Then they'd move on, and she'd remain Lady Love.

And he'd hate himself for the rest of his life if this pervert ended up hurting her.

12

"THEY CAUGHT THE KNIGHT!"

Kelsey nearly dropped the phone when she heard Brian's voice. She'd snatched it up on the first ring, hoping Mitch had decided to call her rather than walk up the stairs and risk another face-to-face argument.

"Kelsey, are you there? I said they caught your secret admirer."

"How do you know?"

"I happened to overhear a conversation going on right now in Jack McKenzie's office."

"Listening at keyholes? Never mind, I know better than to even ask. So, how'd they catch the guy?"

Brian paused and Kelsey knew he was building up the momentum. She could practically hear his excitement in the silent phone line. "Come on," she insisted. "Spill your guts. I know you're dying to."

"Well, one of the secretaries caught him trying to slip a gift into your mail slot. She recognized the blue stationery, confronted him, and he broke down and confessed everything."

Kelsey couldn't believe the man had had enough nerve to stroll right into the station.

"Then what?" she asked, anxious to hear the rest of the story.

"She called McKenzie, and they've been in his office

for the past half hour. I'm sure Jack will be calling you any minute—I wanted to give you a heads-up."

"I appreciate it," she said.

"Don't you want to know who it is?" Brian said, and Kelsey heard the excitement in his voice. "I mean, it turns out this guy's no stranger."

Kelsey paused for a heartbeat, then a name rolled off her lips.

"Edgar."

"How'd you know?" Brian asked, sounding highly annoyed that she'd stolen his thunder. She sat back heavily in her chair.

"You mean I'm right?"

"Yep. It was Edgar. He's confessing everything."

Somehow, Kelsey wasn't surprised. She'd felt all along that the man writing to her was not a threat, but was simply some lonely person indulging in some fantasizing, just as she encouraged people to do on her show. And Edgar fit the bill.

Last night he'd so conveniently been there to drive her home because her car mysteriously wouldn't start, then he'd immediately tried to carry her because of the huge puddle. Looking back, it was so obvious it was all contrived. Edgar was starring in his own hero fantasy and had cast her as the helpless heroine in need of his protection and love. She wondered what he'd done to her car.

"Poor Edgar," she said softly.

Poor me, she thought. Kelsey couldn't believe it was over. Just hours after her relationship with Mitch had blown to smithereens, the reason had been eliminated. It was so unfair, she felt like crying.

"'Poor Edgar' is right. From what I've heard about

his wife, dealing with the station, losing his job and possibly facing prosecution will be the least of his worries."

Kelsey sighed, knowing Brian was right. "I'll tell Jack to forget about the police. I am quite sure I won't be hearing from the 'Knight of my Life' anymore. Edgar was acting out a *Night Whispers*-type fantasy. Now that I know it was him, he probably won't ever want to see me again."

Kelsey finished her conversation, and waited no more than three minutes before the phone rang again. She acted surprised when Jack informed her of what had happened that morning. After he confirmed that Edgar had resigned, she asked him just to let the man go and not involve the police.

She debated with herself about whether to tell Mitch. She was still angry with him, feeling hurt and raw at the fight they'd had that morning. The fact that this whole secret admirer business was over really didn't change anything. Mitch would still want her to quit *Night Whispers*. He'd still want her to change. And she just couldn't.

He didn't deserve to be afraid for her, though. Squaring her shoulders, she walked downstairs and knocked on his door. When he opened it, she noticed a flash of relief crossed his face when he saw her standing there, but as she remained motionless in the hall, he stiffened.

"I just wanted to let you know, so you won't be worried, that the person who's been writing me and leaving me gifts was caught this morning. It turns out he was a lonely man with an overactive imagination who works at the station and never had the nerve to tell me he admired me to my face. He was never a real threat, and has resigned. I'm sure I'll never see him again."

Mitch nodded steadily, feeling greatly relieved. He hadn't been able to think of a single thing all day except how to keep Kelsey safe. Now, it seemed, she no longer needed him to.

"So what now?" she asked softly.

Mitch didn't answer right away. The stalking scare was over, at least for the time being. As for their relationship, he just didn't know.

"You were lucky this time, Kelsey," he said finally. "What about next time? What if the next guy's not just some poor sap with a big imagination?"

She didn't respond. Mitch didn't try to make it easy on her, either. He sensed she wanted to work things out. He probably could have told her they'd move on, forget about it now that this whole mess was over with. But he couldn't let it go. Because deep inside he knew that there would, inevitably, be a next time.

She turned her back to him and walked back up the stairs.

MITCH HAD ABSOLUTELY no desire to attend the Downtown Charitable Society banquet that evening. He was very proud that his articles had drawn attention to the plight of the Chinese girls. But, somehow, attending the elegant affair with all of the rich Baltimore elite who dabbled in charity just didn't appeal to him. What was important was the plaque he'd be bringing home, not hobnobbing with the likes of Amanda Langley's father and his rich board of trustees friends.

And those were the type of men who made up the Downtown Charitable Society.

He heard Kelsey leave to go to work at around seven. She paused briefly outside his apartment door. Wondering for a heart-stopping second if she was going to burst in and demand he make love to her, he admitted to himself that if she did he had no qualms about missing the banquet.

She didn't.

The ceremony was held at a hotel near Harbor Place. Mitch mingled during the cocktail hour, finding himself slipping back into the role of the distinguished, detached writer. As he'd expected, Amanda's father was there, and Amanda was on his arm, looking every bit as lovely and sophisticated as she ever had, in a long beige sheath and a diamond choker.

"Congratulations, Mitch. You look well," she said as she slipped her arm through his and smiled up at him.

"Thank you. I'm surprised to see you here."

"Well," she admitted with a trill of laughter, "I have a confession to make. I made quite certain Daddy and the rest of the board members of the society knew all about the wonders you'd done with your writing. I wanted this for you, Mitch."

She tightened her grip on his arm, pressing her breasts against him, her eyes flashing an unmistakable invitation. Mitch felt more uncomfortable by the minute.

"Let's go take our seats," she said. "I've arranged for you to sit with Daddy and me."

Mitch followed her to the table and spent most of

the evening listening to rich men congratulate themselves on their charitable work. Not one of them looked as if he'd ever actually seen a homeless person, though they all claimed to be terribly concerned about them.

Accepting his award with his prepared remarks, Mitch bowed his head at the perfunctory applause and wished he could make a getaway out the back. The people surrounding him seemed to fade into a blur. They were frivolous and selfish, amusingly catty and condescending. And he knew he could end up just like them.

He felt sick to his stomach.

"Mitch, do say you'll come over for Thanksgiving dinner," Amanda invited. "It was so lovely last year when you joined us. And since you don't have any family nearby, we'd hate for you to be alone."

Mitch thought about the upcoming holidays. For the first time in several years, he pictured himself actually enjoying them. Cooking a turkey, watching a football game, eating so much he could barely move from the table. But when he pictured all these things, it wasn't Amanda's father's mansion he saw. It was his own kitchen.

And Kelsey.

The banquet broke up around eleven, and everyone drifted outside to wait for their limousines. Amanda held on to his arm and urged Mitch to come out for a drink. He never even considered it.

He wanted to be home with Kelsey. Tonight, Thanksgiving night, every night before and after. He loved her. Mitch had admitted to himself that he loved her long before now, but finally the truth of it hit him.

He didn't love Kelsey for the person he wanted her to be. He loved her for the zany, irrepressible, gutsy person she was.

She had been right. In wanting her to give up her show, he'd been asking her to be someone she wasn't. He was basically urging her to do what he had done in his own life: subdue emotion, live logically and by the rules. Doing just that had made Mitch secure financially and socially, but had also left him feeling vaguely unsatisfied, that he was missing out on something. And when Kelsey came waltzing into his ordered home, she'd reminded him of what that was. Passion. Exuberance. Excitement. Laughter. All the rich spices that blended to make a person's life complete—all the flavors he'd tried so hard to make bland through work and ambition.

This evening's glimpse of what his world had been like without her was all it took to convince him he wanted Kelsey to stay exactly the way she was. And to stay with him. Mitch grinned and laughed out loud. He felt like shouting to the moon, but settled for whistling instead.

He was about to make his excuses to Amanda when he saw her eyes widen and her mouth drop open in shock. She stood under a covered awning on a sidewalk outside the hotel and stared out at the street. Mitch followed her stare.

A city bus belching diesel made its way sluggishly up the street to the nearby covered stop. The bus was a typical grimy gray, and only one person waited to board it. Mitch didn't realize what had so captured Amanda's attention until he saw his own face gliding to a slow stop right in front of his eyes.

"Son of a…" he muttered softly, not believing what he saw.

A huge picture covered the side of the bus—a picture of Mitch and Kelsey…or, more accurately, of the pirate and his wench. A photo of Mitch bending toward Kelsey's heaving chest had been blown up to about six feet by six feet and attached to the side of the bus. A caption read "Spend the night with Lady Love on WAJO." Though shown only in profile, both of them were easily recognizable in the provocative shot.

"This is unbelievable," Amanda said shrilly, her voice drawing the attention of everyone else standing nearby. Mitch saw them follow her gaze to the bus and heard the whispers of all those who'd just paid him tribute.

"They can't simply put your face up on the side of a bus. You get a lawyer, Mitch," Amanda continued, her voice getting louder by the second. "You need to sue those people. This is an outrage!"

Mitch watched her squawk, her feathers completely ruffled. He saw the disapproving frowns on other faces around him.

"Yes, it certainly is all wrong," Mitch said, nodding thoughtfully as he stared at the bus.

Not looking at anyone, he grabbed a black marker from the valet stand. He walked the dozen steps to the side of the bus, reached up and quickly drew a small black mustache on his own face on the photograph. Stepping back to survey his work, he nodded at a job well done as the bus ground its gears and pulled away from the stop.

Mitch glanced over his shoulder, grinning at

Amanda's openmouthed stare. "I knew I would have looked better if I'd had time to grow a mustache!"

Mitch laughed out loud at the shocked expressions on the faces of the crowd he'd just spent the evening with. Amanda looked as though she'd swallowed a quart of sour milk. Her father frowned forbiddingly. Mitch felt better than he had in ages.

Whistling, he tossed the pen to the young valet as he walked down the street toward his car.

"HELLO, BALTIMORE, and welcome to another evening of *Night Whispers*."

Kelsey glanced at her notes as she spoke into the microphone.

"Tonight I want to explore relationships. We've all had them, some more successfully than others," she said with a slight laugh.

"Let's not focus on the sweet romance that builds gradually, with emotions leading to physical expression. After all, this *is Night Whispers* you're listening to. Think about those *other* types. You know what I mean—when it starts with raw, physical attraction, builds into desire and fantasy, and finally reaches sensuous, body-rocking lovemaking."

She paused, closed her eyes to let her listeners imagine what she was talking about, then continued.

"No question, the beginning of that type of relationship can involve ultimate pleasure. The anticipation of finally being with someone who makes you hot enough to melt like ice cream on a sizzling summer day is worth the possibility of it going no further than one heated night of passion."

Kelsey forced herself to get her mind off a stormy

October night when she and Mitch had exploded together and changed everything.

"But what happens if there is a next day? A next month, year or decade? When the hot, steamy sex is done, and you're left looking at this person who's consumed your thoughts for a very long time. How do you segue into a real, meaningful relationship? Do you even want to?

"Call me. Let's talk about it. This is Lady Love and you're listening to *Night Whispers* on WAJO."

Kelsey scooted back in her chair and sorted through some discs during a set of commercials. Glancing at the clock, she wondered how Mitch's banquet was going, and wished she'd called in sick and shown up. She would have greatly enjoyed seeing the look on his face if he'd looked up from his speech and seen her standing dressed as his wench under a spotlight!

When Brian cued her, she leaned back toward the microphone. "Welcome back to *Night Whispers*. Tonight we're talking about relationships. Let's skip forward a little, past that initial sensual cloud lovers wrap themselves in. When passion leads to love, how do you make it work? Maybe the person you're passionately involved with isn't right for you, or thinks you're not right for him. How do you move past the obstacles and work on creating something that might actually last?"

The show sped by quickly. Most callers understood exactly what she was talking about and gave tips to others, or else sought commiseration. They discussed marriage and breakups, passion and tenderness. Kelsey wondered why she didn't feel any better, knowing so many other people were in the same boat she was:

in love with someone who thought she was wrong for him and wanted her to change.

"Well, friends," she said as she glanced at the clock, "we're coming to the end of another *Night Whispers.* It's been an interesting night. Do you feel better? I'll be honest. I don't. Sometimes, relationships just stink."

On the other side of the booth, Brian began gesturing. Kelsey noticed there was another phone call. She frowned. She'd already passed the point when she accepted calls, but he looked insistent.

"Well, it seems we have one more late-night caller," she murmured. Punching the connect button on her console, she said, "Good evening, caller, you're on *Night Whispers.*"

"Lady Love? I'm in desperate need of help."

A sudden rush of warmth flooded Kelsey's entire body as she recognized Mitch's voice. "How can I help you tonight?"

"I'm afraid I've gotten myself in a bit of mess with a woman I'm absolutely crazy about."

She smiled, deciding to make him sweat. "Oh? Done something terribly stupid, have you?"

"Uh-huh. Terribly. I made her think I don't want her exactly the way she is. She believes I want her to lose the very qualities that attracted me...until I thought I'd go out of my mind wanting her."

His voice rolled over her entire body and Kelsey nearly curled up in her seat. "And you don't?"

"Absolutely not," he said vehemently. "She drives me crazy, she takes risks, she's outrageous and flamboyant. But, oh, Lady Love, she brings out something in me I thought I'd lost a long time ago."

"What's that?"

A short silence ensued before he replied. "Passion. Passion for life, for pleasure, for everything around us. Sorry to tell you this, Lady Love, but this woman knows more about it than you ever will."

Kelsey laughed softly into the microphone, saying, "Does she know how you feel?"

"Sure, she knows I'm in love with her."

Kelsey sat upright in her chair, bumping her knees on a shelf under the console. *He loved her? He was telling her he loved her? Now? On live radio?*

"Are you sure she knows that? I mean, have you told her that?"

"I've told her in every way possible. I mean, she's very intelligent—she doesn't need things spelled out."

"Yes…she…does," Kelsey muttered tightly.

She heard Mitch's soft chuckle, then he fell silent.

"Sometimes even a woman as sublimely intelligent as yours needs to hear these things said out loud once in a while," she prodded.

"I love you?" he said with a scoffing laugh. "But that just doesn't begin to express it. Besides, like I said, she knows."

Kelsey gritted her teeth. "How?"

"How could she not? She knows me so well. She anticipates my moods, lifts my spirits with one smile, makes me laugh with a word. She can cause me physical pain if she cries. Every minute we spend together is more precious than the previous one. She has awakened me. She has helped me become a man with a future, instead of a man with promise. She's shown me I can have everything I ever wanted, plus all the happiness I ever dreamed of."

ʹTears gathered in the corners of Kelsey's eyes as Mitch spoke.

"She is my first thought every morning, and my last wish every night. She is my past, and she is my future, and she's everything in between."

A long moment of silence hung heavily on the air, and Kelsey could not make her voice work. Tears flowed freely down her cheeks. Finally she breathed deeply and said, "I love you, too."

KELSEY COULDN'T REMEMBER the words she used to wrap up her show. By five after two, she was in her car, driving through the dark streets of Baltimore.

When she arrived at the brownstone, she hurried to the front door and let herself in. The foyer was dark, and she felt a moment of misgiving. Then she sensed him. Her body reacted with the same instinctive longing she always felt when Mitch was near.

"Mitch?"

"I'm here, Kelsey."

And suddenly he was with her, wrapping his arms around her body. Welcoming her home. He lifted her in his arms and carried her into his apartment, kissing her face again and again. Kelsey ran her hands along his shoulders and arms, to be certain he wasn't a dream.

"I love you," he said as he sat her gently on the sofa.

"Well, it took you long enough to say it!"

He laughed aloud and caught her mouth in a deep kiss as he pulled her jacket off and warmed her with his body.

"Did you really mean it?" she asked after they ended their kiss. "You want to make this work between us? Because I want that more than anything, but I'm not willing to let fear drive me away from *Night Whispers*."

He nodded. "I know. I'm always going to worry about you, Kelsey. But I recognize that *Night Whispers* is a part of you."

Leaning down to press a kiss in the hollow of her throat, he whispered, "A very naughty, delicious part."

She savored the rough feel of his cheek on her skin. "I'll be extra careful at work. I won't take any chances."

"We'll deal with whatever happens."

They kissed again, long, deep and wet. Kelsey shifted on the couch, wanting to have nothing between them, particularly her clothing. He slowly began unbuttoning her blouse and she loved how his eyes darkened while he looked at her.

"You're sure you won't mind not having a safe, respectable, responsible, pearls-wearing literary wife?" she whispered.

"Wife?" he asked, looking at her in wide-eyed innocence. "Was that a proposal?"

She pushed him off her until he slid to the floor in front of the couch. Luckily, he landed on his knees.

"No, big guy, it wasn't. I am not going to make *all* the first moves in this relationship!"

"You're not? There's a change," Mitch said with a grin.

She glared at him, but he took her by the hand and kissed the tips of her fingers. "I love you, Kelsey. And I don't just *want* you to marry me, I am begging you to.

After all, who else is going to give me a kick off the straight and narrow when I need it?"

Sliding to the floor in front of him, Kelsey pressed against his body, knees to shoulders, and looked up into his eyes with every ounce of the love she felt for him.

"Sounds like the perfect job for me," she murmured.

He grinned.

"And Lady Love."

_____ Epilogue _____

"GOOD EVENING, BALTIMORE, and welcome to a special edition of _Night Whispers_.

"This is Brian filling in for Lady Love tonight. Our _Night Whispers_ hostess is celebrating a very special event. This afternoon, Lady Love married the man of her dreams and yours truly was in attendance. Ready for the dish?

"First of all, the bride wore white. Now, skeptics among you, stop your tittering. She was utterly gorgeous, a picture of elegance in a floor-length Belgian-lace dress. For those among you who can only see sexiness in red or black lingerie, stretch your brains and visualize the power of purity. High collar, long sleeves, perfectly fitted to her figure, with pearl buttons running from her neck all the way down her back. Imagine the anticipation of a groom slowly slipping each button free and I'm sure you'll understand the appeal.

"Speaking of the groom, if there was ever a man born to wear a formal black tux, it's him. Ladies, he looked like a fantasy man, tall, lean and powerful. And the look of adoration on his face when he saw our lady walking down the aisle was something no one in that church will ever forget.

"The ceremony was traditional, and everything went smooth as clockwork, though the mother of the bride cried enough to leave black streaks down her cheeks. Always remember, please, waterproof mascara for these occasions.

"During the vows, steam came out of the bride's ears when the minister said the word 'obey.' The groom and the best man, the bride's brother, laughed loud enough to be heard in the back of the church. Lady Love didn't realize they'd put the minister up to it until he winked at them. The groom got a sharp-knuckled little punch in the upper arm before he swept his bride into his arms for an oh-so-passionate kiss.

"The reception was held at a hotel near the Inner Harbor. In keeping with Valentine's Day tradition, red velvet bows decorated every table and the hall was packed with well-wishers.

"There was not a dry eye in the place when Lady Love stepped out onto the dance floor with her father, and they were joined by the groom and the bride's mother. The two couples shared the moment, eventually changing partners and then coming together for a group hug at the end. Another Kodak moment.

"Of course, the real fun started after the bride and groom departed for their honeymoon to the Caribbean. One of the ushers, an old college buddy of the groom, had too much to drink and got a little too friendly with the maid of honor. Her boyfriend, one of the other ushers, decked the guy, knocking him into the champagne fountain. The best man, who'd been fending off every unattached woman in attendance, broke up the fracas and was last seen disappearing into the elevator with a lovely redhead.

"We have to pause now, for a commercial break. I've got lots more juicy details on Lady Love's wedding day, so be sure to come back for more *Night Whispers.*"

Look for a new and exciting series from Harlequin!

HARLEQUIN *Duets*™

*Two **new** full-length novels in one book, from some of your favorite authors!*

Starting in May, each month we'll be bringing you two new books, each book containing two brand-new stories about the lighter side of love! Double the pleasure, double the romance, for less than the cost of two regular romance titles!

Look for these two new Harlequin Duets™ titles in May 1999:

Book 1:
WITH A STETSON AND A SMILE
by Vicki Lewis Thompson
THE BRIDESMAID'S BET
by Christie Ridgway

Book 2:
KIDNAPPED? by Jacqueline Diamond
I GOT YOU, BABE by Bonnie Tucker

2 GREAT STORIES BY 2 GREAT AUTHORS FOR 1 LOW PRICE!

Don't miss it! Available May 1999 at your favorite retail outlet.

HARLEQUIN®
Makes any time special.™

If you enjoyed what you just read,
then we've got an offer you can't resist!

Take 2 bestselling love stories FREE!

Plus get a FREE surprise gift!

Clip this page and mail it to Harlequin Reader Service®

IN U.S.A.	**IN CANADA**
3010 Walden Ave.	P.O. Box 609
P.O. Box 1867	Fort Erie, Ontario
Buffalo, N.Y. 14240-1867	L2A 5X3

YES! Please send me 2 free Harlequin Temptation® novels and my free surprise gift. Then send me 4 brand-new novels every month, which I will receive months before they're available in stores. In the U.S.A., bill me at the bargain price of $3.12 plus 25¢ delivery per book and applicable sales tax, if any*. In Canada, bill me at the bargain price of $3.57 plus 25¢ delivery per book and applicable taxes**. That's the complete price and a savings of over 10% off the cover prices—what a great deal! I understand that accepting the 2 free books and gift places me under no obligation ever to buy any books. I can always return a shipment and cancel at any time. Even if I never buy another book from Harlequin, the 2 free books and gift are mine to keep forever. So why not take us up on our invitation. You'll be glad you did!

142 HEN CNEV

342 HEN CNEW

Name	(PLEASE PRINT)	
Address	Apt.#	
City	State/Prov.	Zip/Postal Code

* Terms and prices subject to change without notice. Sales tax applicable in N.Y.
** Canadian residents will be charged applicable provincial taxes and GST.
   All orders subject to approval. Offer limited to one per household.
   ® are registered trademarks of Harlequin Enterprises Limited.

TEMP99   ©1998 Harlequin Enterprises Limited

 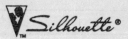

 **HARLEQUIN®**
Makes any time special ™

 WIN A DREAM

In celebration of Harlequin®'s golden anniversary

Enter to win a *dream!* You could win:

- A luxurious trip for two to *The Renaissance Cottonwoods Resort* in Scottsdale, Arizona, or

- A bouquet of flowers once a week for a year from **FTD**, or

- A $500 shopping spree, or

- A fabulous bath & body gift basket, including **K-tel**'s *Candlelight and Romance* 5-CD set.

Look for **WIN A DREAM** flash on specially marked Harlequin® titles by Penny Jordan, Dallas Schulze, Anne Stuart and Kristine Rolofson in October 1999*.

 FTD

RENAISSANCE. COTTONWOODS RESORT SCOTTSDALE, ARIZONA

 K·TEL